STACY GREGG grew up training her bewildered dog to showjump in the backyard until her parents gave in to her desperate pleas and finally let her have a pony. Stacy's ponies and her experiences at her local pony club were the inspiration for the *Pony Club Secrets* books, and her later years at boarding school became the catalyst for the *Pony Club Rivals* series.

Pictured here with her beloved Dutch Warmblood gelding, Ash, Stacy is a board member of the Horse Welfare Auxiliary.

Find out more at: www.stacygregg.co.uk

The Pony Club Rivals series:

PONY CLUB RIVALS
Showjumpers

STACY GREGG

HarperCollins *Children's Books*

This book is dedicated with grateful thanks to Stan Govender,
John Harman, Keith Barclay, Beverley Sweeten-Smith,
Melissa, Lisa and the wonderful team at St Marks

www.stacygregg.co.uk

First published in Great Britain by HarperCollins *Children's Books* in 2010
HarperCollins *Children's Books* is a division of HarperCollins*Publishers* Ltd,
77–85 Fulham Palace Road, Hammersmith, London, W6 8JB

2

Text copyright © Stacy Gregg 2010

ISBN 978-0-00-733344-8

Stacy Gregg asserts the moral right to be identified
as the author of the work.

Typeset in 11.5/20pt Palatino by Palimpsest Book Production Ltd,
Falkirk, Stirlingshire
Printed and bound in England by Clays Ltd, St Ives plc

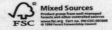

Chapter One

As Georgie Parker stepped aboard the plane, she felt like a total imposter. She was about to enter a world that was far too glamorous for a girl from Little Brampton – a tiny horsey village in the middle of rural Gloucestershire. Up until a couple of months ago when she had first arrived at the Blainford Academy, the closest she'd ever come to being taken anywhere by a boy was when Adrian Baxter had given her a double to the shops on the handlebars of his bike. Now, here she was, being whisked away on a private jet, about to spend the mid-term break with the impossibly gorgeous James Kirkwood.

Try to act casual, Georgie told herself. *Pretend you spend all your time on board private jets.*

"Sorry we got stuck with the little plane today," James

apologised as he threw their luggage into one of the overhead lockers. "Dad and The Stepmom are using the big one. I guess we'll have to make do!"

Georgie took in the sleek interior of the jet and couldn't keep up her act any longer. "Ohmygod, James," she said as she sat down on one of the enormous white leather seats. "This is totally amazing!"

"Do you want a drink?" James said as he walked to the back of the plane and opened a wall cabinet to reveal a fridge. "There's lemonade, Coke or juice."

"Juice, please," Georgie said. She peered out the window of the plane. The airstrip was located at the back of the school grounds, so from here she had a rear view of the red brick Georgian buildings of the academy. To the right, she could make out the roofline of the stable blocks in the distance, where earlier that morning she'd said a tearful goodbye to Belladonna.

She wouldn't see her horse again until after the mid-term break. "You don't know what it's like," Georgie had complained to her best friend Alice as she locked the loose-box door for the last time. "You're so lucky – getting to take Will home with you for the holidays."

"Oh, please!" Alice had laughed. "You cannot seriously tell me that you would rather stay here with Belle than go away with James for five days?"

No one had been more surprised than Georgie when James Kirkwood had asked her to spend mid-term break with him at his family's mansion in Maryland. James was a whole year ahead of Georgie and even amongst the world-class riders at this exclusive equestrian boarding school he stood out. He was a gifted showjumper, handsome and talented, the shining star of the Burghley House polo team, and heir to the Kirkwood millions.

The only downside of spending the holidays with James was his sister. Kennedy Kirkwood was a first year at the school, just like Georgie. From the moment that Kennedy discovered Georgie had topped the UK auditions for Blainford she had been desperately competitive with her. And after losing dramatically to Georgie on the cross-country course during mid-term exams, Kennedy's dislike of her rival had reached epic proportions. Georgie had spent the last week of school virtually in hiding so that she could avoid Kennedy and her gang – the showjumperettes. But so far James hadn't mentioned his sister. There was still no sign of her and Georgie was beginning to hope that maybe Kennedy wasn't coming.

"Here you go, an OJ cocktail before take-off." James passed Georgie her juice and threw himself down in the seat next to her, sighing as he looked at his watch.

"Hey, Lance!" he called out.

In the cockpit, the pilot put down the newspaper he was reading.

"Yes, Mr Kirkwood?"

"What's the weather like in Maryland?"

"Clear as a bell, Mr Kirkwood," the pilot replied. "It should be a nice flight. We're just waiting on the others and then we'll depart."

"What others?" Georgie asked nervously. Her question was answered with a dramatic whoosh as the gull-wing doors of the plane opened and a girl with glossy red hair wearing a white sundress and gold sunglasses stepped on board. She took one look at Georgie and her expression soured.

"What is *she* doing here?"

"I told you I was bringing someone," James said, "and you've kept us waiting – which is typical!"

"It wasn't me this time." Kennedy Kirkwood dropped her bags before collapsing elegantly into one of the plane's plush leather seats. "It was Arden. She took forever to pack."

Georgie couldn't believe it. Spending the break with Kennedy was bad enough without the equally toxic socialite Arden Mortimer in tow!

It got even worse when a pointy-faced blonde girl entered the cabin weighed down with several large Louis Vuitton bags.

"Kennedy! Can't you tell the pilot to turn off those appalling plane engines? They're ruining my blow dry!" The cut-glass British accent belonged to Tori Forsythe – the third member of the showjumperettes. She struggled up the stairs, while Arden Mortimer breezed in afterwards, her glossy dark mane tied back in a high ponytail and nothing but a make-up compact and a lip gloss in her hands.

"Where are your bags, Arden?" Kennedy asked.

"Andrew's got them," Arden said airily as she took a

seat. Behind her on the stairs a boy dressed in a Ralph Lauren mint green polo shirt was grunting as he struggled with Arden's matching luggage.

"Man, Arden," the boy groaned as he threw the bags down at her feet, "why am I carrying your stupid bags? And what have you got in here anyway?"

Arden gave him a dark look. "Andrew, you might be able to survive on your pastel polo shirt collection, but some of us need to accessorise to get through a five-day break."

Andrew Hurley ignored this and strode over to help himself to a Coke out of the fridge, then he turned to James.

"Dude," he frowned, refusing to acknowledge Georgie, "you didn't tell us you were bringing her."

"*Her* name is Georgie," James said coolly. "Georgie – you know Andrew Hurley, right? He's in Burghley House with me."

"Hi, Andrew," Georgie smiled at him.

"Whatever," Andrew groaned as he slumped into his seat at the back of the plane.

The last passenger to board the plane was a boy with

black wavy shoulder-length hair. His name was Damien Danforth. Georgie had seen him around the school with the rest of the second-year polo set. At school he dressed in the same uniform as the rest of the Blainford boys – black jodhpurs, brown boots and a navy shirt – but somehow managed to carry himself with a poetic flair that the others didn't possess, wearing his navy shirt intentionally a size too large and leaving the buttons undone so that the cotton billowed as he strolled about the quad. Damien had a way of speaking, as if each word was an enormous effort. He had a transatlantic accent – neither American nor British, but somewhere in between.

"James," he said as he shoved his bags up into the locker, "I couldn't find my hunting stock. I'll have to borrow one of yours..." Then he turned and spotted Georgie. "Hello! I didn't realise Taylor Swift was coming with us."

Georgie felt suddenly self-conscious about the fact that Alice had helped her to style her hair into ringlet curls instead of her usual plain blonde ponytail.

"Damien, this is Georgie Parker," James said, "and

before you say anything else rude to her, you should know that she's my guest."

"I wasn't being rude!" Damien looked aghast. "I adore Taylor Swift!" He threw himself into the seat in the aisle opposite Georgie and leaned over to her.

"So Taylor, sweetheart, where did you come from?"

"Umm," Georgie was thrown. "I'm from Little Brampton, in Gloucestershire."

"Georgie is British eventing royalty," James added. "She's Ginny Parker's daughter."

"Is that true?" Damien looked impressed.

"Well, yes," Georgie nodded, "but only the bit about my mum being Ginny Parker."

"Oh, good," Damien said with relief. "We've already got Kennedy on the plane – we don't need another princess onboard."

"Shut up, Damien!" Kennedy threw the pillow off her seat at him.

"Hey, no fighting! Buckle up, everyone," James grinned. "We're taking off."

As they'd been talking, the jet had done its short taxi to the end of the grassy airstrip and the engines were whining and thrumming. Suddenly Georgie was thrust back in her seat as the plane gathered speed, until it struck that moment of pure freedom as the wheels lifted off the ground and they were airborne in the clear blue sky, bound for Maryland.

Georgie thought it was ironic that James had introduced her as eventing royalty. Royalty implied being privileged, but that was the last thing that Georgie felt. Her mother, Ginny Parker had died in a tragic accident on the cross-country course four years ago and since then it had just been Georgie and her dad. Their country life was hardly one of luxury and Georgie had been forced to sell her beloved black pony Tyro because she couldn't afford to board him with her at Blainford. Instead, she had been allocated one of the Academy's horses to ride. At Blainford, riding a school horse tainted you with a whiff of impoverishment – a fact that Kennedy was only too keen to point out.

Georgie hadn't been exactly thrilled about her assigned horse at first either, but now she adored

Belladonna. She was a headstrong mare, but such a beauty with a jet-black mane and tail and coat of dark mahogany. Georgie was really beginning to bond with Belle. Their relationship felt so natural. Which was more than she could say about James. She wasn't even sure where she stood with him. Were they officially dating? The way he looked at her now with those startling blue eyes was totally unnerving.

"Regretting coming with me?" James asked.

"No," she lied.

"Ah, but you haven't met my parents yet," James deadpanned.

"I'm sure they're not that bad," Georgie said.

"No," James replied, "they're worse. Don't worry, I'm sure they'll love you. Dad used to be a showjumper when he was at Blainford, so all you need to do is mention that you've made the team for the House Showjumping."

"Your dad must have been proud when you made it into the Burghley team," Georgie said.

"You'd think so, wouldn't you?" James gave her a wry smile. "It's hard to tell with my father."

The House Showjumping was an annual event at

Blainford and just before mid-term break the try-outs had been held for the school teams – Georgie and James had both been chosen to represent their boarding houses.

When Georgie got back to school, there would be showjumping training to contend with – as well as a mountain of schoolwork. Despite being an equestrian academy, Blainford didn't cut students any slack when it came to academic subjects like English and Maths. But it was cross-country class with Tara Kelly that really had Georgie stressed out. In their half-term exam, Georgie had finished halfway up the class rankings and so had avoided elimination. However, Tara had already promised that the next half-term would be even more challenging than the first.

"Tara is a total dragon. Her class is a nightmare," James said. "Although you seem to cope."

"I'm still alive, if that's what you mean," Georgie replied.

"All you cross-country students are the same," James said. "You act like it's so important…"

"But it is!" Georgie said. "James, I came here to become

an eventer and Tara is the best instructor in the business. Being in her class matters to me more than anything."

As the pilot had promised, the weather was good all the way to Maryland. Almost exactly an hour after they had taken off, the plane began its descent. They came down through the clouds and then suddenly the skies were clear and they were close enough for Georgie to see the tops of the trees and cattle grazing on velvet-green pastures.

"That's the house down there," James said, leaning over and pointing out the grey shingled roofline of a massive country mansion.

Alice had warned Georgie that the Kirkwoods owned the grandest house in Maryland, but even so, Georgie hadn't really expected anything on this vast scale. The Kirkwood property was like an English country estate. Spanning out around the house in all directions were vast, formal gardens. From above, the hedges and topiary created an elaborate maze, dotted with fountains and statuary. Beyond the gardens, James pointed out guest cottages made from the same grey stone as the main house, and stable blocks for the horses, polo fields and dressage arenas.

Georgie could hear the clunk beneath the belly of the aircraft as the plane lowered its landing gear. She looked out of the window at the green, grassy airstrip rushing up at them and watched as a handful of black-faced sheep grazing the pasture below them scattered out of their path.

Seconds later the plane struck the ground with a vigorous bounce. There were a few more bumps and thuds as they bounced across the airstrip and then the plane was turning around and heading towards the hangar at the rear of the mansion.

As the others disembarked, Georgie reached for her bag.

"Leave it," James instructed. "You don't have to carry your own bags around here."

If the Kirkwood mansion had looked like a grand affair from the sky, it was no less daunting when you were standing on the doorstep. From the front, the building had even more of a stately air, with dark ivy growing vigorously up the walls almost to the roofline and a beige pebbled forecourt at the front entrance, with a large fountain for the cars to drive around.

James rang the bell and a few moments later the front door swung wide open. Georgie was confronted with an attractive woman in a dark navy suit, her hair pulled back in a tight elegant bun that accentuated her wide blue eyes. She looked nothing like James, but Georgie wasn't surprised by this. After all, James had told her that he had a stepmother.

"Georgie," James said, "this is Frances."

"It's a pleasure to meet you, Mrs Kirkwood," Georgie said. Trying her hardest to be polite, she extended her hand to shake, but the woman made no effort to take it. Georgie thought that perhaps a curtsy might be more appropriate. She withdrew her hand and dipped down at the knees, doing a little bow. As she rose up again she saw that the woman was staring at her in utter bewilderment.

Kennedy gave a snicker. "Frances is our maid," she informed Georgie as she barged past with Tori, Arden and the boys behind her. "The stepmom doesn't answer the bell around here."

"Where is Patricia?" James asked Frances.

"Your stepmother is on her way back from Paris," the maid replied. "And your father—"

She was interrupted by the deep sonorous boom of a hunting horn that made Georgie spin around. Across the green lawns of the Kirkwood gardens, darting in between bushes and leaping over hedges, came the fox hounds. The pack was running with their tongues lolling out and tails held erect. They must have been at the end of a run because their tan, black and white coats were covered in burrs and mud.

When they reached the elegant fountain in the forecourt the hounds began to leap straight in, some of them lowering themselves to sink down beneath the water and cool off, others standing on all fours in the shallow fountain, lapping away at the water. The horn sounded again and Georgie saw a man appear astride a magnificent grey hunter. He wore a red jacket that signified that he was the master of the hounds. He had the horn in one hand and with the other he kept a light grasp on the reins as he rode directly down the middle of the carefully mown lawn, jumping metre-high topiary hedges as if they weren't even there.

"Ohmygod!" Georgie was stunned.

"I know!" James nodded. "Just as well Patricia isn't here. She'd give him a telling-off for galloping across the front lawn like that."

The man cantered the horse across the pebbled forecourt and pulled his mount up right in front of Georgie and James. When he vaulted down to stand beside them, he towered over James. He was as solidly built as his hunter and his red hair was greying at the temples beneath his velvet riding hat. He pulled off his brown leather gloves and shook hands with James in a brisk fashion.

"The hounds had a good run today," the man said. "They're in good shape for the hunt tomorrow. I assume you're joining us at ten to throw off?"

"Wouldn't miss it," James confirmed.

"Hunting?" Georgie was horrified.

"You don't hunt?" The hunt master frowned.

"I can't even believe you'd ask me that!" Georgie said. "Chasing after a poor little fox on horseback and killing it like that! It's cruel and barbaric."

"Now wait a minute…" the man tried to say.

But Georgie was in full swing. "I think it's pathetic. All those dogs set against one poor fox as some sort of ghastly entertainment."

"But—" the hunt master tried again.

"It's outlawed in Britain, you know," Georgie continued. "I'd have thought America would ban it too – like any civilised society."

This last sentence was something Georgie had heard in Social Studies the week before and she was quite pleased to be able to use it to bold effect.

The hunt master sighed. "Are you finished?"

Georgie nodded emphatically.

"Right," the hunt master said. "Firstly, they're not called dogs. They must always be referred to as hounds. Secondly, we are not hunting foxes. No fox has ever been hunted on Kirkwood land – we hunt an aniseed lure and no animals are killed for our pleasure. And as for being civilised, I find it is always good manners to greet your host before you begin to rain torrents of abuse on them for crimes they have not committed."

Georgie felt her stomach do a flip-flop. She'd just made a major mistake.

"Georgie," James sighed, "I didn't get the chance to introduce you. This is my father."

The huntsman extended his hand. "A pleasure to meet you, young lady," he said in a tone that indicated it was anything but. "I'm Randolph Kirkwood."

Chapter Two

Mrs Kirkwood arrived home from Paris late that afternoon. Georgie noticed that James and Kennedy greeted their stepmother in the same detached manner that James had used with his father on the front lawn, as if they were mere acquaintances rather than family.

Patricia Kirkwood swept into the house wearing high heels and a sharply tailored black suit, her jet-black hair swept up into a chignon and lengths of gold chains roped around her neck. She was a consultant for a major fashion house in Paris and divided her time between her office in France and the Maryland mansion.

"Working in fashion must be so glamorous," Georgie said when they were introduced.

"It's a juggling act," Patricia replied. "I can be in

jodhpurs on Friday riding across our estate, and back in haute couture gowns on Monday choosing fabrics for the new collections."

Arden and Tori, who were both fashion-obsessed, made sure they were sitting next to Patricia at dinner and spent the whole time quizzing her about fashion trends.

Kennedy looked outrageously smug when Mrs Kirkwood announced that she would be taking her stepdaughter to see the runway shows next season. James however, seemed less impressed.

"I think she hates it really," he told Georgie as he watched his stepmother flitting in and out of the dining room, her mobile phone glued to her ear, throughout the meal. "All the endless runway shows and high heels, the air kisses and back-stabbing. She works for Fabien, that French designer who wears the ridiculously big shoulder pads? Patricia is his muse. Apparently he adores her and can't design the range without her – but the rest of his staff can't stand her. They call her Hamburger Patty because she's American. I think the only reason she keeps doing the job is to avoid us. She's hardly ever home and when she is, she's out hunting."

It seemed that hunting was an obsession for the Kirkwoods. Patricia had returned from Paris to prepare for the hunt the next day and during dinner she was constantly distracted with preparations for tomorrow's activities, snapping orders at various members of staff.

Mr Kirkwood, meanwhile, never appeared at dinner at all. "He's down at the kennels with the hounds," Frances told Mrs Kirkwood when she asked after her husband. Georgie was relieved to hear it. After her misguided outburst she didn't really fancy sitting down to dinner with him.

"Why didn't you tell me he was your dad?" she groaned to James.

"I was having too much fun watching you," James grinned. "Dad was totally stunned to have someone disagree with him. It doesn't happen very often."

Neither Mr or Mrs Kirkwood seemed to show much interest in Georgie – or in any of the teenagers, including their own children.

"This house is so big," James told Georgie, "I came

home once for mid-term break and it took them the whole week to realise I was even here!"

He'd meant the story to be funny, but Georgie thought how awful it would be to come back to an empty mansion and for no one even to notice you were home.

James had given her a quick tour of the ground floor before dinner and Georgie had been overwhelmed by the luxury and size of the mansion.

"Don't leave me behind," she told James as she trailed after him. "I may never find my way out of here on my own."

"Guests have been known to disappear," James agreed with a wink.

The maze of corridors was so confusing that when it was time to go to bed, Georgie had to rely on Frances as a guide. Georgie followed the clack-clack of the maid's court shoes on the parquet floor as she led the way. At the end of the main hall they climbed the grand staircase that led to the west wing of the house. Georgie's guest room was the fifth on the left and had its own bathroom and dressing room.

"You'll find some of Kennedy's old hunting clothes in

the wardrobe," Frances said as she turned down the bed. "She told me you would need something to wear for tomorrow."

Like the other rooms in the house, Georgie's guest room was completely over the top. It was as if several interior designers had been hired at once and had fought it out with no clear winner. The chairs were cloaked in animal prints – leopard, zebra and tiger stripes, the cushions were floral, the furniture was French antique and there was baroque wallpaper hung with Chinese tapestry. If this was how Patricia Kirkwood decorated her house, Georgie shuddered to think what she might put on a catwalk!

In the dressing room she searched through jods and jackets hanging on the rails, choosing herself a suitable outfit for tomorrow. Georgie had never hunted before, but she knew that young riders were meant to wear tweeds and thankfully there were several suitable things to wear here. She selected a buff tweed hunting coat and cream jodhpurs, both of which looked like they would fit, then she rummaged around in the cupboard and found a hunting stock that was the same shade of cream as the jodhpurs. Georgie decided she would wear her long black boots to complete the outfit. Then she laid them all carefully on a zebra-print chair, ready and waiting for her.

A heavy mist hung over the estate the next morning. Georgie looked out her bedroom window and was greeted by the magical sight of horses and riders in scarlet coats milling about on the front lawn. By the time she had showered, pulled on her hunting clothes and raced downstairs there were already nearly a hundred riders gathered on the pebble forecourt, their horses breathing steam from their nostrils as they waited for the hunt to throw off.

The horses were classic hunters, stocky types with thick strong legs and chests that were deep through the girth. Georgie loved the way they had been clipped so that it looked as if their top and bottom halves actually belonged to two entirely different horses, joined together in the middle.

The riders all looked far more dressed up than Georgie had expected and despite the early morning hour they were drinking port, sipping away at the stirrup cups that were handed to them by servants carrying silver trays. Patricia Kirkwood, dressed in a black velvet hunting coat and lace cravat, was holding court amid a group of shrill and overbearing riders who were behaving more like they were at a cocktail party than a hunt.

"Avert your eyes!" There was a whisper in Georgie's ear and she turned around to see Damien Danforth standing behind her. "If you stare at one of those gorgons directly you could turn to stone," he deadpanned.

"Watch it – they might hear you!" Georgie was taken aback.

"Who cares?" Damien sniffed. "If you had to spend ten minutes in a room with Patricia's awful friends you'd see I'm simply telling the truth."

He gave Georgie a dark look. "I blame you, you know. You British were the ones who invented all this hunting nonsense and made it seem classy. Now every nouveau riche moron in Maryland wants to join the Kirkwood hunt. Honestly, I don't think half of them know one end of a horse from the other."

"You're exaggerating," Georgie smiled.

"I'm not!" Damien insisted. He pointed to a rider seated

on an enormous dark brown hunter. "That's Heatley Fletcher," he said. "Local lawyer and multi-millionaire. Do you notice anything odd about his horse?"

Heatley's big brown hunter stood out with its hot-pink leg bandages.

"A bit flamboyant," Georgie admitted.

"You know why?" Damien whispered. "Heatley is famous for turning up at a hunt and not even recognising his own horse. He's had to be asked twice this season to dismount because he got on the wrong one. Finally his groom came up with the solution of putting coloured bandages on Heatley's hunter so he won't embarrass himself any more."

"Of course," Damien added, "the bandages don't stop Heatley from falling off. He usually plummets at the first hedge because he can't actually ride."

"He can't ride?" Georgie was horrified. "Then what's he doing hunting?"

Damien sighed. "Being invited on the Kirkwood hunt is like being invited to the *Vanity Fair* party at the Oscars. So they all come. And they all drop like flies at the first spar."

"You seem to know this place and the Kirkwoods pretty well," Georgie said.

Damien gave her a long-suffering look. "James and I met at boarding school when we were nine years old. He's one of my best friends," he paused, "although I often wonder how James turned out the way he did..."

"Talking about me?"

It was James. Georgie had no idea how long he'd been standing there behind them.

"I was just telling her the Kirkwood secrets," Damien said.

"Don't," James warned him. "You'll put her off!" Smiling at Georgie, he clasped his arms possessively around her waist. Georgie was shocked by this sudden public display of affection.

"Come on," he said. "Let's go to the stables and I'll introduce you to your horse."

The stables turned out to be utterly beautiful. Patricia Kirkwood had clearly never thought of bringing her fashion sense outside so the interior was mercifully untouched. The stable block had bare flagstone floors and high-vaulted ceilings with wooden beams.

James led Georgie to one of the loose boxes on the far right-hand side. "You've been given Belvedere," he told her, unbolting the top of the stall door.

Belvedere was a heavily built brown horse, part-draught with a broad white blaze and a face that was so immense and solid that the throat lash of his bridle could barely fit around his broad cheeks. Still, his eyes were bright and kind, and he met Georgie's gaze keenly. His ears pricked forward as she approached him and took his reins.

"He's lovely," she said. "He has such an honest face."

"Belvedere's a reliable jumper," James assured her as he legged her up. "I would have preferred to put you on something with a bit more class like Tinkerbell, but Dad said she's not for first-timers."

Georgie suspected that what Mr Kirkwood really meant was that he didn't consider her good enough for his best horses, so he'd stuck her with a draught horse. Still, she wasn't complaining. She really liked Belvedere, although sitting astride him felt weird after riding Belle. His heavy physique bulged out beneath her, the barrel of his belly forcing her legs to stick out like she was doing the splits.

As she lumbered back across the lawn trying to get used to Belvedere's cumbersome trot, Georgie caught sight of the showjumperettes. Kennedy and her friends were mounted up on elegant, well-bred hunters and all of them wore sleek black riding coats with frilled stocks at their throats and top hats instead of helmets. Next to them on her draught horse in her borrowed country tweeds Georgie looked like an unsophisticated hick. She could see from Kennedy's smirk that this had been her intention all along.

"Interesting choice of outfit," she said to Georgie. "Beige is really your colour, isn't it?"

"Thanks, Kennedy," Georgie replied sarcastically. "Oh, and by the way, Abraham Lincoln called – he wants his top hat back."

Kennedy's expression turned fierce. "You obviously know nothing about hunting. If you get in Dad's way today, he'll feed you to the hounds."

"Calm down, Kennedy," James said, "I was just about to tell her the rules."

He smiled at Georgie. "There's really only one rule. My dad is the master of the hunt and you must never overtake him on the field. Those other guys with him in red coats are Dad's henchmen – the whippers-in, and the field masters. They'll try and boss you around, but don't worry, just do as I say and no matter what, always stick with me. OK?"

Georgie didn't have time to reply. Randolph Kirkwood raised the horn to his lips, giving a long, low blast. Then he set off at a brisk trot, the hounds following obediently at the heels of his great, grey hunter. The pack scampered across the pebbled driveway, heading to the right of the house towards a low stone bridge that crossed a small stream, leading out into the pasture beyond. They kept alongside their master in tight formation until they reached the field, and then they began to fan out, casting for the scent.

Two hounds to the far left of the field began baying, and soon the others had joined in their howling chorus. Randolph Kirkwood gave another toot on his horn to alert the riders behind him and then the hunt was off and galloping.

The hounds covered the ground far more swiftly than Georgie had anticipated. They kept pace with Randolph Kirkwood's hunter, who flew the first obstacle, a clipped hedge at the far end of the field, without hesitation. Dedicated to the pursuit of the scent, the hounds squirmed and thrashed their way through the hedge. Several men in red coats followed, along with Mrs Kirkwood, who jumped the fence with expert finesse.

With the competent riders over the hedge, the rest of the field surged in a mad rush. Just as Damien had predicted, Heatley Fletcher was one of the first to fall. Georgie saw his big brown hunter skid to a halt in front of the hedge so that Heatley flew over his mount's neck, landing face-first in the mud.

Heatley's horse caused a collision with three other riders, two of whom also promptly fell off. Georgie watched the pile-up in astonishment.

"Total carnage!" Damien said with a grin as he rode up alongside her.

"I told Dad we should ride at the front," Kennedy whined. "Now we're stuck behind the losers."

"Out of the way, please!" James was yelling at the riders dithering about and blocking the path in front of the hedge. He rode his liver chestnut, a pretty mare named Bambi, at an astonishingly gutsy gallop. If things went wrong and he came to grief it would make for a very nasty fall, but James' confident style made it clear that he had no intention of either stopping or falling. Damien, Andrew, Kennedy, Tori and Arden all followed his lead, pushing in to take their turns over the hedge until only Georgie was left. She looked at the hedge. It was a fair-sized jump, probably a metre high. "Hurry up, Georgie!" James called to her. "We're going to lose the hounds at this rate!"

Georgie took a deep breath and shortened up the reins. "Come on, Belvedere," she pressed the big brown hunter on and rode him hard at the hedge.

At the last minute Belvedere tried to swerve away, but Georgie held him steady with her legs, growling to urge him on again. The hesitation meant they were now on a bad stride and Georgie considered pulling the horse off. Then she remembered what her old riding instructor

Lucinda Milwood always said at moments like this: "When in doubt, kick on!" And so she did, giving a firm dig with both heels. Belvedere pulled himself together, knowing that his rider meant business. He chipped in a last-minute stride and managed to get them over the hedge with Georgie securely on his back.

That first jump gave Georgie a jolt of adrenalin and she felt her confidence come upon her in a rush. She stood up in her stirrups in two-point position, keen and ready for the next obstacle.

At the next jump, a low dry-stone wall, Georgie didn't need any encouragement and popped Belvedere over it on a lovely forward stride. She was enjoying herself now, feeling the wind in her face, the thunder of hooves beneath her.

James was right beside her, but the rest of the hunters were quite spread out. Mr and Mrs Kirkwood, the scarlet-coated huntsmen and hounds were far ahead in the distance. There were about a dozen hunters in hot pursuit of the front runners, and then behind them came the stragglers, many of them sporting muddy patches on their breeches and hunting jackets.

As they approached the next fence, a large hedge, Georgie was squaring up to take her turn when James called her name and peeled off in front of her, making a sharp turn and riding away from the other hunters.

Remembering his instructions, Georgie pulled hard on the left rein to turn Belvedere away from the hedge and set off in pursuit.

They were galloping towards a small glade of trees – Georgie guessed that James must have an alternative route in mind. Straight ahead of them was a four-barred post and rail fence. James didn't even slow down. He rode Bambi over it without hesitation and Georgie felt her blood racing as she did the same. Belvedere's massive frame made it feel like she was riding an elephant, but there was no doubt that this horse could jump!

Over two more fences they went – a low fallen log and another quite large hedge. She heard the noisy crackle of branches as Belvedere dragged his hooves through the top of the hedge like an experienced hunter. Then she heard the low call of the huntsman's horn and looked back over her shoulder. They had left the hunt far behind. The hounds had veered in totally the opposite direction and were getting even further away. Still, she figured James must know what he was doing. He knew the hunt fields like the back of his hand, so surely he must have a plan.

Ahead of her, James had ridden into a clearing in the middle of the glade. He pulled Bambi abruptly to a stop and flung himself out of the saddle. Georgie saw him dismount and immediately assumed the worst. If he was getting off his horse then Bambi must have thrown a shoe.

"James!" She cantered Belvedere up alongside and quickly vaulted off. "Are you all right? Is Bambi OK?"

"She's fine," James said.

'Then why did you dismount? What's wrong?" Georgie took the reins over Belvedere's head and led him over to where James and Bambi stood.

Both of the horses were sweaty and heaving. She could feel her own heart racing from the exertion of the gallop. "Why are we here...?" she began to ask. And then suddenly he was standing so close to her that she could no longer tell if it was her own heart racing or his, pressed up against her.

"I think I can smell aniseed," was all she managed to squeak out, as he moved his face even closer and met her lips with a kiss.

Chapter Three

*I*t had quickly become obvious that James had no intention of rejoining the hunt. Instead, he took Georgie on a tour of the estate. They followed a bridle path, riding through woodlands and open fields, and by lunchtime they were starving and miles away from the Kirkwood mansion.

Georgie thought she was going to faint from hunger when James finally led the way through a gate out on to the main road and they rode along the grass verge to the junction where a petrol station, general store and diner stood on the corner.

They tied the horses up there and bought burgers and fries and sat down to eat beside their horses on the grass. Georgie was horrified by James' habit of dipping his fries in his chocolate thickshake.

"It's a trick I learned at Blainford," he admitted. "The food in the dining hall is so bad, you learn to improvise."

On the way home they cantered over the fields, jumping low hedges and spars rather than bothering to stop and open the gates. It was almost dark when they finally made it back to the stables. Georgie took Belvedere to his stall and had started to untack when James stopped her. "You know we've got staff who do that," he told her. "Leave him with the grooms and come up to the house."

Georgie shook her head. "But I want to do it." She couldn't stand the thought of handing over her horse for someone else to do the dirty work. Exhausted as she was, she didn't want to abandon Belvedere, leaving someone else to mix his hard feed and rug him up. "I'll groom him myself," she told James.

"Suit yourself." James looked mildly amused, as if the idea had never occurred to him. Georgie realised at that moment that the Kirkwoods treated their horses as if they were just pieces of equipment – like a motorbike or a tennis racquet to be put away at the end of a game, rather than a living creature. The horses in this stable virtually had their price tags hanging off them. Which made it even more insulting that Mr Kirkwood had refused to give her Tinkerbell to ride. He didn't trust her to ride his horse in the same way that he wouldn't trust a one-armed juggler with a Ming vase.

"I'll see you back up at the house," James said. "I'd steer clear of the conservatory if I were you – that's where Patricia and Dad will be having their post-hunt drinks. A lot of bores with mud on their breeches telling their lame war stories." He smiled at her. "I'll be in the games room hiding from them."

Grooming Belvedere took Georgie longer than she'd expected and somehow all the mud and sweat that had been on the big, brown gelding managed to transfer itself on to her in the process. Her jods were covered in muck and she had the worst case of helmet-hair she'd ever had in her life. It was in this bedraggled state that Georgie entered the mansion. She had planned to go upstairs and get changed, but when she heard Mr

Kirkwood's voice on the landing she detoured immediately and headed to the games room in search of James.

In the games room Kennedy Kirkwood was playing pool. She had taken off her top hat and coat and was leant over the table dressed in her breeches and white blouse, her frilled hunting stock still tied at her throat. Beside her, also holding cues, were Tori, Andrew and Damien.

"And what happened to you on the hunt field today?" Damien raised an eyebrow and gave her a cheeky look. "You seemed to vanish."

"We should be so lucky!" Kennedy commented as she took her shot and managed to sink the black ball mid-game by mistake.

Andrew swept his arm across the table to clear the remaining balls. He didn't even acknowledge Georgie's presence and seemed determined to pretend she wasn't there as he racked up for another game.

"Where is my brother anyway?" Kennedy glared at Georgie. "You didn't actually manage to lose him on the hunt field?"

"He told me he was going to be in here," Georgie said. "I haven't seen him since he left the stables…"

The large French doors in the games room opened straight out to the gardens and the sound of giggling and splashing could now be heard right outside.

"Well we know where he is now," Damien said, peering out the window. "He's out by the fountain with Arden."

Georgie felt herself turn strangely cold. It was almost nightfall outside. Why was her boyfriend hanging out in the garden?

Her suspicions got even darker when James and Arden tumbled in through the French doors, giggling and panting, as if they'd been playing chase. James was still in his riding clothes, but Arden had got changed into a stunning emerald green chiffon dress. Her hair was blow-dried perfectly and tied back loosely and she'd taken off her strappy high heels and was carrying them delicately dangling in one hand, as if she'd just stepped out of *Vogue*.

"Georgie!" James seemed surprised to see her. "Finished mucking out the stables then?"

Georgie tried to take his teasing in her stride. "Yeah, well, Belvedere is a big horse – it takes a while to groom all of him," she said. Then she added, "What were you and Arden doing outside?"

"None of your business!" Arden said airily, dropping her shoes on the floor and collapsing dramatically into a chair.

James gave Georgie a grin. "We weren't doing anything," he said. "Just hanging out."

Frances entered the games room at that moment to announce it was time for dinner. Somehow Arden managed to manoeuvre herself closer to James as they walked to the dining room and snaffled the seat beside him at the table. She then spent the entire meal whispering in his ear, winding Georgie up even more. Unfortunately the Kirkwoods served dinner in six courses and it took forever. All the time, James hardly even bothered to look at Georgie and by the time dessert was being served she felt close to tears. Unable to stomach any more of Arden's flirting, Georgie said she wasn't hungry and left the table. She was heading for her room when she heard footsteps behind her in the hallway.

"Georgie! Wait!"

It was James. He ran to catch up with her. "Going to bed early?" he asked.

"I'm just tired, I guess," Georgie said unconvincingly.

"Don't go," James said. "We can go back to the games room."

"Why don't you go and hang out with Arden?"

The words were out of her mouth before Georgie could stop herself. She looked at James' face, and saw a brief smile cross his lips.

"Don't be like that, Georgie," he said sweetly. "We had fun today, didn't we?"

Georgie wanted to say that it had been more than fun – it had been one of the best days she'd ever had. "I'm so sorry," she blurted out. "It was an amazing day. It's just... I've never felt like this about anybody before and I—"

And then she had to stop talking because, for the second time that day, James Kirkwood was kissing her.

As the light poured in through the curtains the next morning, Georgie's first thought was of James Kirkwood and that kiss. As she got up and began to dress she heard the sound of the jet engines. It sounded as if a plane was taking off from the airfield behind the mansion. She didn't give it too much thought at the time, and headed down to the dining room where Frances was serving breakfast. She'd dished herself up some scrambled eggs and was about to sit down to eat alone when Damien Danforth burst in through the dining-room door. He was dressed in jodhpurs and long boots and his cheeks were ruddy from the fresh air.

"Hello!" he said, looking rather surprised to see Georgie. "Are you still here?"

"Of course I'm still here!" Georgie replied. "Where have you been?"

"Oh, we've been for a morning ride," Damien said, heading straight over to the buffet. "Frances!" he yelled out. "Got any of those field mushrooms?"

A moment later the rest of the party came rushing in. Andrew as usual didn't bother to speak to Georgie, Tori and Arden came in giggling, and then Kennedy followed them. When she saw Georgie, her face dropped.

"Are you still here?"

Georgie frowned. "Yes! Still here. Why does everyone keep asking me that?" She looked behind Kennedy through the open doorway. "Where's James? Is he with you?"

A look of dark delight appeared on Kennedy's face. "You don't know?" she said. "He didn't tell you?"

"What are you talking about?" Georgie asked.

Kennedy purred with pleasure, "Oh, it's too fabulous!"

Georgie suddenly felt awfully vulnerable. Kennedy clearly knew something that she didn't.

"James has gone," said Damien.

"Gone where?" Georgie was confused. Was he down at the kennels with his father? Out on the estate?

"He's gone to New York with his dad," Damien said. And then he added in a gentler tone. "I'm sorry, Georgie, I thought he'd taken you with him."

"Well, when will he be back?" Georgie asked.

"He's not coming back," Kennedy said. "He's gone with Dad and then he's going straight to Blainford." She gave Georgie a look of mock pity. "Looks like he's left you behind."

Georgie couldn't believe it. "But there are still three

more days until we're due back at school. He can't just leave me…"

"He just did," Kennedy said. "This is so typical of James. Dumping you and making it our problem!"

Georgie would have burst into tears, but she didn't want to give Kennedy the satisfaction. Instead, she put down her breakfast plate and left the room. She was halfway down the hall when she heard Damien calling after her.

"Are you OK?" he asked as he ran to catch her up.

"Not really." Georgie shook her head, still struggling to hold back the tears. "Why did he go off like that without saying anything?"

Damien shrugged. "He was in a weird mood this morning. He said he had to get out of here and he'd tell me all about it when we got back to school. Then he left."

Back in her room, Georgie sat down on the bed in despair. How could James abandon her at his house with Kennedy and her stuck-up friends? It was so unbelievably awful she couldn't help but think there must be some mistake. She couldn't believe that James would do this.

"That's right, he's gone to New York with his father," Patricia Kirkwood confirmed. Georgie had looked everywhere and finally found James' stepmother in the library. However, Mrs Kirkwood seemed to show scant interest in Georgie's predicament.

"It's just…" Georgie hesitated, "Well, he brought me here and now he's gone and, umm, I'm still here."

Patricia Kirkwood stood up and began to rearrange flowers in a vase on the mantelpiece. "So I see," she said flatly. "You're welcome to stay of course," she added. "I'm sure you can get a lift back to Blainford on the weekend with Kennedy and the others when they go."

"Thank you," Georgie managed to stammer out, "only I wasn't expecting to be, well, abandoned by James."

Patricia Kirkwood froze, and suddenly her focus became quite resolutely fixed on the vase in front of her. "To be honest, Georgina, we weren't really expecting James to bring home a girl… like you…"

She paused to withdraw a dead rose from the vase. "There's a certain calibre of girl that is suitable for the Kirkwood household. I think perhaps James was forgetting his position when he asked you here in the first place."

Looking back, Georgie would think of endless biting comebacks that she wished she had said to Patricia Kirkwood. But at the time, her jaw literally hung open in shock. No wonder the Kirkwoods had seemed aloof. They'd never wanted her here, because they didn't think that she was good enough for James!

Patricia Kirkwood pulled out another dying rose and then turned on her heels and walked briskly out of the room. Georgie was reeling! What was she going to do now? She was stuck here without James, unwelcome and yet unable to leave for another three long unbearable days. Then she would be forced to get on that plane and fly back with Kennedy and her sidekicks, gloating and taunting her the whole way.

Back upstairs in her room she curled up in a ball on her bed, feeling utterly lost and alone. Why had she come here? She should have taken Alice up on her offer and gone to her house instead.

Alice! *Of course.* Georgie leapt off the bed and searched in her bag. With trembling fingers she dug through her things until she uncovered her mobile phone, and scrolled through to find Alice's number. Alice lived in Maryland too, not far from the Kirkwoods.

Georgie listened to the dialling tone on her phone. *Please pick up, Alice!* she pleaded silently. She held her breath and waited and then, just as she was about to give up, there was a familiar voice at the other end of the line.

"Georgie!" Alice's cheery voice almost made her burst into tears with relief. "Are you having a good time at the fabulous Kirkwood Mansion?"

"Not so much," Georgie admitted. There were gasps of horror and disbelief from Alice as Georgie told her the 'highlights' so far.

"So where are you now?" Alice asked.

"I'm hiding in my bedroom," Georgie said. "Which is probably where I'll be staying for the next three days until I can leave."

"No," Alice said firmly. "You won't be. I'm coming to get you right now. Get packed. I'll be there as fast as I can."

It didn't take Georgie long to throw her things in a bag. Once she was ready, she went back downstairs and told Frances she was leaving. She couldn't wait to get out of this place. But there was one final goodbye that she had to say before she went.

"Belvedere," Georgie cooed as she unbolted the door of the gelding's stall and stepped inside. "I've got something for you."

At the sound of Georgie's voice, Belvedere came closer. Georgie reached out her hand and the big brown hunter spied a carrot in the outstretched palm. He stepped forward and used his soft lips to nuzzle the treat from her, crunching the carrot with his enormous jaws.

"Thank you for being such a super horse," Georgie told him, patting his broad muzzle before slipping back out the stable door. "Bye, Belvedere," she said sadly. "You were the nicest of all of them."

As she walked through the gardens towards the house, Georgie half hoped that she might see a car in the driveway, but no one was here to collect her yet. Instead, she saw Kennedy standing on the steps to the front door with Arden and Tori. They were holding racquets and waiting for Tori to do up the laces on her tennis shoes.

"We're going down to the courts," Kennedy told Georgie. "We'd have asked you to come – except we didn't."

"That's OK, Kennedy," Georgie replied. "I'm leaving in a minute anyway."

Kennedy looked taken aback. "What do you mean?"

At that moment there was the low rumble of a lorry engine and heavy wheels crushing the pebbles on the driveway. Then the deep honk of a horn sounded as the Duprees' horse transporter pulled into view.

"Georgie!" Alice was waving frantically out of the passenger window as her big sister Kendal swung the wheel of the massive lorry to turn it around the fountain.

"I'd love to stay and chat," Georgie said, amused by the look of total shock on the showjumperettes' faces, "but my ride is here."

She looked over at Alice, who was beaming as she swung open the door. Georgie threw her bag in and climbed onboard. "See you back at Blainford," Georgie said, slamming the door. She squeezed in next to Alice, doing up her seatbelt as Kendal put the lorry into gear.

"Go round the fountain once more!" Alice begged her sister. Kendal's skinny arms swung the wheel hard as she did a 360-degree turn to circle the fountain for a second time while Georgie and Alice raised their hands to the window and pretended to wave like the Queen as they bid the stunned showjumperettes goodbye.

Chapter Four

Kendal Dupree was a senior at Blainford and the older sister by three years – which in her books meant she should be in charge. Alice Dupree, however, had other ideas.

"Hey! Don't touch the CD player!" Kendal snapped. "I'm listening to that!"

"It's old ladies' music!" Alice pouted.

"It's Joni Mitchell," Kendal replied. "She's one of the coolest female singers ever."

"Boring old hippie," Alice grumbled. "Put on the new Foals album!"

She reached out a hand towards the CD player, but Kendal grabbed her wrist to stop her.

"Ow! Let me go!"

"Alice! Stop it. I'm trying to drive." Kendal flicked her

long blonde hair back out of her eyes and focused on the road ahead. "I'm warning you. Touch it again and you're dead."

Alice scowled at her big sister, her dark eyes half hidden beneath her jet-black fringe. "You're lucky you're an only child!" she said pointedly to Georgie. "It's awful having a big sister."

"Hey!" Kendal shot a sideways look at Alice. "You dragged me out on this crazy rescue mission. How about a bit of gratitude?"

"Thank you, Kendal," Georgie said with sincerity.

"As if you had anything better to do!" Alice mumbled.

The bickering between the sisters carried on pretty much like this all the way to the Dupree ranch. Georgie marvelled at how the sisters constantly taunted each other without actually meaning anything by it.

In between arguing, Alice quizzed Georgie, until she had heard the whole story of what had happened with James.

"I always knew he was toxic," Alice said. "He's so vain and arrogant."

"He's not," Georgie insisted. "Not once you know him."

She didn't know why she was standing up for James or why, despite what he'd done, she still felt a desperate need to see him again. All she knew was that she wasn't ready to hate James Kirkwood. Not just yet.

The Dupree house was two-storeyed and painted white with a massive kidney-shaped swimming pool set into the lawn. Kendal swung the wheel of the lorry and eased the vehicle down the tree-lined driveway towards the front of the house. Georgie expected Kendal to pull up and stop, but she kept on driving.

"Mom and Dad are down at the stables," Alice explained.

As they arrived outside the stable block, two enormous American Staffordshire terriers bounded out, followed by a small but yappy Jack Russell.

"Hey, Spike!" Alice said, swinging open the lorry door and leaping down to pat the brindle-coloured Staffordshire terrier, while the black and white spotted one leapt up to get her attention. "That one is Lulu," Alice said, "and the Jack Russell is Ralph."

Even though Ralph was the smallest, he did all the barking. He'd obviously made enough noise to announce their arrival because the Duprees came out of the stables a moment later to greet them.

"You must be Georgie," Mr Dupree said, reaching out his huge bear paw to clasp her hand, a broad smile on his face. "I'm Charlie. Lovely to have you here. Alice has told us so much about you. I hear both of you girls made the House Showjumping team this term!"

"Hi, hon!" Mrs Dupree had a Maryland accent that was much stronger than Alice and Kendal's. She was tanned and lean like her husband and wore her black hair back in a ponytail. She had the same bubbly personality as Alice and she didn't hesitate to give Georgie a vigorous hug.

"Where's Cherry?" Alice asked.

"She's working the horses out back," Mrs Dupree said and smiled at Georgie. "Do you need anything to eat, hon? Maybe some lemonade?"

"No, thanks," Georgie said, "I'm fine."

"Well come out to the arena then," Mrs Dupree said, "and see what you think of this five-year-old that Cherry convinced us to buy."

The Duprees were the sort of family that Georgie's old instructor Lucinda would have classified as "true-blood horsey". It was so clear that all of them adored horses, and more than that, they understood them too.

Cherry, the oldest of the Dupree sisters, was a Blainford graduate who was now riding the professional showjumping circuit. Like Alice and Kendal, she was lean and delicately built like a ballerina. The five-year-old in question was a Hanoverian called Doodlebug. He was sixteen-two and had the temperament of a volcano. When Georgie arrived, Cherry was having trouble settling him down and he kept doing little bucks as he went over the jumps. Cherry didn't look at all perturbed by this, even though she was jumping him bareback!

"Oh, Cherry doesn't like to use a saddle on the young ones," Mrs Dupree told Georgie. "Doodlebug doesn't have the strength in his back yet – he's too young, too green."

Georgie was stunned. The jumps in the arena were over a metre high and Cherry was taking the horse over all of them. How on earth did she manage to stay on?

"Cherry jumps Grand Prix without a saddle," Mrs

Dupree said matter-of-factly. "She used to get into no end of trouble at Blainford, always being told off for riding bareback!"

While Mr Dupree rearranged the jumps with the dogs gambolling along at his heels, the rest of the family watched Cherry from the sidelines.

"Doodlebug's on the forehand." Alice frowned as she watched Cherry collect him up.

"She needs to sit back," Kendal pointed out. "That'll make him put in that extra stride before the jump."

Mrs Dupree relayed their observations to Cherry, who acknowledged them with a cheery smile. "Charles," Mrs Dupree called out to her husband. "Can you put a canter pole in front of the oxer to help Doodlebug take off?"

"Cherry has six horses that need work at the moment," Mrs Dupree told the girls. "I'm sure she'll be glad of an extra hand now that you're here too, Georgie."

Georgie didn't need to be asked twice. Genuinely happy, she and Alice headed off to the stables to find themselves a horse.

For the next two days the girls spent nearly all their time down at the arena riding Cherry's young jumpers. Cherry insisted that they ride bareback, which took some getting used to at first, but eventually Georgie found that she could hold her normal position over the fences, almost as if the saddle was invisible beneath her.

Afterwards they would come back up to the house and mess about, teaching the dogs to leap over the living-room furniture. Incredibly, Mrs Dupree didn't seem to mind. "Having you girls home for the holidays is like having a hurricane come to stay," she would laugh as Ralph, Spike and Lulu crashed into the couch and sent sofa cushions flying.

At mealtimes the conversation invariably revolved around horses and Georgie felt like she'd learnt more about showjumping at the Duprees' dinner table than she had in her whole life before. She loved hearing Cherry's stories about the professional showjumping circuit.

"Is Miss Loden still teaching Natural Horsemanship classes?" Cherry wanted to know.

"She's on sabbatical," Georgie told her. "She's gone to

some island in the Bahamas to do research on the wild Abaco horses."

"I learnt to jump bareback in her class," Cherry said. "Some of the other teachers were uptight about it, school rules and that, but Miss Loden was cool."

With a name like Cherry, Georgie had been expecting the oldest Dupree sister to be a redhead and had been shocked the first time she took off her helmet to reveal dark blonde hair. She had the same tanned skin as Kendal and was naturally beautiful, just like her sisters.

"Oh, my! Cherry broke hearts when she was at Blainford," Mrs Dupree told Georgie when she was in the kitchen on Saturday afternoon helping to peel potatoes for dinner. Mrs Dupree saw the look on Georgie's face and quickly added, "Not that there's anything clever about being a heartbreaker, Georgie. Alice told me a little about what happened with that Kirkwood boy. You did nothing wrong, hon. You trusted him and he let you down. You can go back to that school tomorrow with your head held high."

It was such a kind thing to say, Georgie found herself on the verge of tears. It had been so long since she'd had her own mum around, and even though Mrs Dupree already had three daughters who were quite demanding, she'd made Georgie feel like there was more than enough room for her in the family too.

The last days of the mid-term break passed all too quickly and on Sunday morning, Georgie helped Alice and Kendal load their horses up the ramp of the lorry. Then the girls said their goodbyes and prepared to make the long drive back to Blainford. It was the first time that Mr and Mrs Dupree were letting Kendal drive there by herself.

"Here," Alice said, as they waved goodbye out the window and cruised up the driveway, "put this on." She thrust a CD at her sister.

"Over my dead body," Kendal replied. And so the squabbling began that would take them all the way to Route 64, and the long straight highways that led back to Lexington and Blainford Academy.

When they finally arrived just before dinnertime on Sunday, students were pouring back into the school. Horse lorries, as vast and glamorous as super-yachts, lined the Blainford driveway as they deposited horses and pupils, their sleek state-of-the-art designs looking strangely out of place beside the Georgian brick front of the school.

As Kendal parked the lorry at the far end of the driveway Georgie spotted Daisy King and Emily Tait waving to them.

Daisy had been Georgie's toughest competition on the eventing circuit in Gloucestershire. It was obviously too far for Daisy to go home for the mid-term break so she had stayed at the school and her New Zealand room mate, Emily Tait, had done the same. Both the girls were in Badminton – the same boarding house as Alice and Georgie. The houses at Blainford were named after famous international horse trials – there were six of them: Badminton, Burghley, Lexington, Stars of Pau, Adelaide and Luhmuhlen. Friendships and allegiances at the school were frequently defined by which house you were in.

Burghley House was located on the driveway and was the nearest building to the main college. It was a boys' boarding house and considered by the arrogant polo set to be *the only* house to be in. James Kirkwood was in

Burghley, of course, and so were Damien Danforth and Andrew Hurley. The head prefect of Burghley was Conrad Miller, who made a special point of picking on Georgie – giving her fatigues (Blainford's version of detention) on her very first day.

Of all the boys' houses, Georgie liked Luhmuhlen the most. Two of her best friends from eventing class – Cameron Fraser and Alex Chang – were in Luhmuhlen. Lexington House had most of the Western boys and Matt Garrett, an Australian eventer who could be annoyingly full of himself.

The girls' houses tended to mirror the boys so, just as Burghley was the house to be in for the polo boys, Adelaide had the same reputation for showjumping girls. The showjumperettes – Kennedy, Arden and Tori – were all in Adelaide. The uncoolest house was Stars of Pau, which tended to accommodate dressage riders and students who chose the stranger Blainford subjects like carriage racing or horse vaulting. Georgie had a few friends in Stars of Pau including Isabel Weiss, a dressage rider who had been in her cross-country class before she got eliminated after the mid-term exam.

"Badminton House is the best one," Alice had told Georgie on the first day they'd met. Badminton's residents were very international. There were students from the USA, but also riders like Emily Tait and Georgie who came all the way from opposite ends of the world. Already in the few short weeks that they had been together, the Badminton girls had begun to feel like family. Even Daisy was like a sister – in an annoying, competitive sibling-rivalry way.

"Why were you in Alice's horse lorry?" Daisy asked as Georgie jumped down from the cab. "I thought you were spending the mid-term break at the Kirkwoods with James?"

"I was. It's a long story…" Georgie began.

"James dumped her," Alice said. "She called me and I came and got her."

"All right, maybe not such a long story." Georgie sighed.

"You're kidding!" Emily couldn't believe it. "What does Alice mean, he dumped you?"

"Well, I don't know for sure. Maybe it was a misunderstanding," Georgie said. "He went with his

68

dad to New York and he just sort of, well, he left me behind."

"Tell us about it over dinner," Emily said. "We're just on our way up to the dining hall."

"We need to unload the horses first," Alice said. "Give us a hand?"

While the two sisters led their horses towards the stables, Emily, Georgie and Daisy followed behind, carrying their tack. As they walked, Georgie told the unabridged version of the story, beginning with her arrival at the Kirkwood mansion and ending with Alice and Kendal coming to her rescue.

"I wish I'd seen the look on Kennedy's face when the truck turned up," Daisy said. She wasn't a Kennedy Kirkwood fan either.

At the stables, Alice put Will in his loose box. Georgie was dying to say hello to Belladonna, but the mare wasn't in the stalls – she was out grazing in one of the school's paddocks.

"Come back and see her later," Emily said. "If we don't go now we'll miss out on dinner."

They walked briskly from the stables, back up

the driveway. Ahead of them they could see the main building of the school, its red brick front with white columns and three turret rooms on the top floor that jutted up into the sky out of the red-shingled roofline. A vast stone archway in the front of the building led into a courtyard where a large square lawn, known as the quad, was bordered by broad footpaths and red-brick buildings on every side. The building on the furthest side of the quad contained the dining hall. Even though they were in a rush, the girls didn't risk cutting directly across the quad. Georgie knew from bitter experience that only prefects and school masters were allowed to set foot on this hallowed piece of lawn.

"We're going to be just in time," Emily was saying as they entered the dining room through the heavy wooden double doors. "Dinner finishes at seven-thirty and..."

Suddenly she stopped speaking and silence fell over the group. Ahead of them in the queue were the boys from Burghley House waiting to be served by the cafeteria ladies. And there he was, laughing and talking to his friends as if nothing was wrong. He was the one person that Georgie had been dying to see. But now she was actually in the room with him she found herself wishing the ground would swallow her instead. It was James.

Chapter Five

*E*ver since James had left her at the Kirkwood mansion, Georgie had been imagining the moment when they would meet again. She'd mentally rehearsed their reunion a hundred times. James would beg her forgiveness, and Georgie would respond with a light, witty comment to prove that he hadn't broken her heart and she was still the one in charge.

In her dreams, maybe, but this was reality. They stood there in the dining hall surrounded by the Burghley House boys – Damien, Andrew and, worst of all, vile Conrad Miller – and James wasn't apologising. He wasn't even looking at her.

Georgie stepped back into the queue between Emily and Alice and said nothing. Maybe she could pretend that she hadn't seen him? She didn't have the nerve to approach him with the other boys there.

Then she heard Conrad Miller's voice booming across the hall. "Hey, Kirkwood! Your girlfriend is behind you!"

There were snickers from the Burghley boys and then Conrad called out to her, "Want to come hunting with me sometime, Georgie?"

Andrew Hurley followed his lead in a silly high voice. "Oh, James, I've never felt like this about anyone before…"

Georgie's blood ran cold, her eyes fixed in horror on James. He'd told them! He'd told them everything. How could he?

James caught her eye then looked away, that stupid lopsided grin on his face, as if this were all a joke.

"Georgie." Alice was standing right next to Georgie. "Just ignore him and get your food. He's so not worth it."

The School Formal was a Blainford tradition at the end of the first term. "Tickets are going to be available at the front office next week," Mrs Dickins-Thomson told the school at assembly on Monday.

"Make that a ticket for one, please," Georgie groaned under her breath.

"Make that two tickets for one!" Alice muttered back. "And at least you had a boyfriend – even if he did turn out to be evil."

Mrs Dickins-Thomson, the Blainford headmistress, was a thin, horse-faced woman, with very erect posture and a no-nonsense manner. She ended the assembly with an update on the House Showjumping competition.

"The competition is next month," Mrs Dickins-Thomson said. "The house teams were chosen before term break and your coaches will be advising you shortly on training schedules. Please check your house noticeboards for details, if you are in the squad."

Georgie was the first out of her seat when assembly was over, dashing through the doors. By the time Alice caught up with her, she was halfway around the quad.

"Geez, Georgie," she complained. "I've never seen you this keen to get to German!"

"I'm not!" Georgie hissed. "Hurry up!" She wanted to get to the safety of the classroom where there was no chance of accidentally bumping into James Kirkwood. He was a second year at Blainford so fortunately they didn't share any classes.

Kennedy, however, was unavoidable. She strode into Ms Schmidt's German class with Arden and took her usual seat, not even bothering to look at Georgie. It seemed like Kennedy had called a kind of truce, but as Ms Schmidt began the lesson she raised her hand. "Ms Schmidt?"

"Yes, Kennedy?"

"What is the German word for 'being dumped'?"

Ms Schmidt was confused. "You mean the word for rubbish? Like a landfill?"

"No." Kennedy cast Georgie a sly glance. "I mean like, if a boy dumps you."

Arden burst into giggles.

"I don't see the use for this phrase," Ms Schmidt said humourlessly. "And I don't see what is so funny."

"Get Georgie to explain it to you," Kennedy said, at

which point the showjumperettes all collapsed into fits of giggles.

Georgie struggled on through Maths and English, finding it increasingly hard to focus with Kennedy constantly making snide comments.

"I hate the fact that Kennedy's loving this so much," Alice said as they walked towards the dining hall for lunch. She looked at Georgie, who had turned white at the prospect of entering the dining hall again. "Don't worry," Alice said reassuringly, "it'll be OK."

As they walked in, Georgie's eyes did a quick scan of the dining room, relieved to see that the polo boys must have been and gone already.

The dining hall was in one of the oldest buildings on the Academy grounds, a vast space with high vaulted ceilings and dark wood-panelled walls decorated with ancient black and white photos of previous Blainford pupils. The hall was filled with long trestle tables, each of which sat eight pupils at a time. Like any high school cafeteria, the students divided themselves into cliques.

But the cliques at Blainford were different to those of a normal school – the students were split into strictly horsey social groups.

Georgie looked at the table right beside the lunch queue and saw Tyler McGuane and the rest of the Westerns hanging out together. Tyler was a good-looking boy with shoulder-length blond hair and a fringe that was so long you could barely make out his eyes. He owned a palomino Quarterhorse called Maybelline and was in the youth team for the Calgary Rodeo circuit. Next to him sat his best friend, Jenner Philips, his long black hair tied back as usual. Jenner could rope a calf in under eight seconds, and he'd been the under-sixteen bareback bronc champion two years in a row at Calgary.

Beside the two boys sat Bunny Redpath and Blair Danner, never seen without chewing gum in their mouths. Bunny rode a pinto mustang, while Blair had a sorrel gelding that perfectly matched her chestnut hair. She had qualified for a scholarship for Blainford because she was a national junior champion at barrel racing.

At the next table sat the dressage geeks from Stars of Pau house – Isabel Weiss, Mitty Janssen and Reina Romero.

Although serious and swotty, they were gifted riders. Isabel, who wore her blonde hair in a plait that wrapped around her head like an alice band, was from Frankfurt in Germany. Mitty, who was from Holland, was Isabel's best friend. The third member of their group, Reina, was Spanish and rode a long-maned grey Andalusian called Destino. Although some of the other riders considered dressage to be a 'sissy option', Isabel and Mitty had thoroughly proven their courage by joining Tara Kelly's cross-country class at the start of term. Isabel had been the first student to be eliminated, but Mitty was doing rather better than everyone expected on her big Swedish Warmblood. Georgie smiled at Isabel and Mitty and gave them a wave as she headed for her own table where the others were waiting.

The eventers – Georgie's gang – sat at the same table in the far left corner of the room. These riders were the core of the first-year eventing class. Friends and yet rivals at the same time, they were all driven by the same goal, to secure top ranking in cross-country by the end of the year. The palpable tension amongst the group arose from an unavoidable fact: not all of them would last the year.

The cross-country class was renowned for its high drop-out rate. Riders fell by the wayside with broken bones and shattered nerves – and if that wasn't bad enough, there was also their teacher to contend with.

Tara Kelly was the head of Blainford Academy's eventing department and taught the cross-country class. She had a policy of 'sorting the wheat from the chaff', which meant that for the first term she put the class through a gruelling elimination process and got rid of any students that she didn't think were good enough.

Elimination was brutal, but Tara's argument was that it was for the pupils' own good. Cross-country was not your usual subject. It was a deadly game and by term two, when the jumps began to get really scary and dangerous, it was vital that only the very best riders, who had the courage and skills to cope with riding at such a high level, remained.

The riders at Georgie and Alice's table included Georgie's fellow Brit Daisy King. Georgie had been hoping that she and Daisy might have developed a common bond since they were both English, but if anything the rivalry between them had become even more intense at Blainford. Next to Daisy was her Badminton House room mate, Emily Tait. Emily was a quiet, unassuming rider, and yet she'd managed to ride her big black Thoroughbred, Barclay, to victory in the mid-term exam point-to-point, trouncing all the others to come home in first place.

Beside Emily sat the French rider, Nicholas Laurent. Confident to the point of arrogance, Laurent had been a superstar back home in Bordeaux. After all, he'd made the national junior eventing team by the age of *eleven*. Laurent's greatest competition, at least when it came to conceit, was undoubtedly Matt Garrett. The Australian rider had a swagger to his riding style and was annoyingly brilliant across country. Georgie wanted to dislike him, but was constantly impressed by his instinctive cunning and sheer bravado.

Georgie's best friend in the cross-country class, apart from Alice, was Cameron Fraser. He was a Scottish rider who had the most amazing natural 'stickability' on a horse. He could ride through a water complex, lose his reins and stirrups and still emerge out the other side on his horse's back. Cameron shared a dorm room with the rider sitting beside him, Alex Chang. Despite being on the Chinese junior eventing team, Alex spoke with a very pronounced English accent. His mother was a diplomat and Alex had learnt to ride in Oxfordshire. He'd brought his own horse with him to Blainford, a grey Anglo-Arab gelding called Tatou.

Georgie had a secret crush on Tatou, who was quite easily the prettiest horse in the whole of Blainford. If she were to ride any horse instead of Belladonna then it would definitely be Alex Chang's stunning dapple grey. And as for secret crushes, late in the boarding house the night before, Emily had confided to Georgie that she had a crush on Alex himself!

The eventing clique was tightly knit. They all knew everything about each other, as Georgie was beginning to realise.

"So what's this about you and Kirkwood?" Cameron launched straight in as soon as she sat down. "Do you want me to have a go at him?"

"No, thanks, Cam," Georgie smiled awkwardly.

"Probably just as well," Cameron admitted. "I'm a

totally rubbish fighter. The one and only time I've ever been in a scrap was with my best mate back in Coldstream, and I ended up with a black eye."

"That's nothing to be ashamed of," Georgie said.

"My best mate was called Annabel," Cameron pointed out.

Georgie laughed. "It's OK, Cam," she said. "I'm not going to ask you to defend my honour."

"Not if you fight like a girl," Alice agreed. She had a better suggestion. "We should quarter him."

"What do you mean?" Georgie asked.

"You know, like in medieval times, how people were hung, drawn and quartered?" Alice explained. "We'd just do the last bit, the quartering. All you have to do is tie a horse to each of his arms and legs and then get them to gallop in four different directions and he'll get ripped into four different quarters."

"Gross!" Emily said.

"But effective," Alice replied, looking pleased, "and we could use our own horses."

"Well," Cameron said as he finished his lunch. "I'd love

to stay here talking about torture, but it's time we all went and experienced it instead."

He was right. Lunchtime was over and they were due at their next class. It was time for their lesson with Tara Kelly.

Chapter Six

After almost a week off, Georgie had been excited about getting back on Belle again – but when she saw the mare her heart sank.

"She's like a hippo," Georgie moaned as she brought Belle inside and tied the mud-caked mare up at the hitching posts next to Alice's horse, William, and Cameron's big piebald, Paddy. "It's going to take forever to get her cleaned up."

Now that the rainy weather was setting in and the fields were muddy, Georgie had been expecting to keep Belle boxed in the stables. But there were too many horses at Blainford for everyone to be assigned loose boxes, and so it had been decided that the school horses would continue to graze outdoors.

The divide between the pupils who were rich enough to afford to keep their own horses at Blainford and those who weren't had never been more brutal. Georgie would have to deal with a muddy horse for months until the weather improved.

Underneath the winter rug, she was surprised to see how furry Belle had become in less than a week. Autumn days were shorter and the decrease in sunlight had stimulated the growth of the horses' winter coats.

Even with her thick layer of winter fuzz, you could see how finely built and beautiful Belladonna was. She was a deep red bay with a jet-black mane and tail and black points, and a stunning white heart-shaped marking on her forehead.

When Georgie had first met the mare she had been struck by how much Belle resembled the Warmblood mare Boudicca, who had once belonged to her mother. And it turned out there was a good reason for this – Belle was Boudicca's foal. As Georgie got to know Belle better, she could see the differences between the two horses. Although she shared Boudicca's distinctive markings and exquisitely shaped head, physically Belle was much finer, with a lighter frame. Belle was also half-Thoroughbred. Her sire had been a racehorse and his bloodlines gave her a delicate refinement and, in theory, a swiftness that Boudicca had never possessed. However, being half-Thoroughbred also accounted for the young mare's hot-headedness. The mare had talent, there was no doubt about it, but she wasn't an easy ride.

Georgie had only just managed to get the mud off when she realised that they were due in the arena already. She'd been hoping to tidy up Belle's tail and pull her mane, but there simply wasn't time. The riders were already assembling in front of the cross-country jumps, waiting for Tara Kelly, who was walking across the field towards them.

For someone with such a formidable reputation, Tara was a slight figure. If she were a horse then she would undoubtedly have been a Thoroughbred – all lean limbs and fine bones. Tara was dressed today in pale cream jodhpurs, a crisp white shirt and a padded beige gilet with her shiny walnut-brown hair tied back in a ponytail.

"I hope you all had a good mid-term break and a chance

to recover after the last exam." Tara said briskly, addressing the line-up.

"I know that many of you have House Showjumping commitments, and bearing that in mind I have decided not to schedule an end-of-term exam."

There was a ripple of relief among the riders until Tara added, "Instead, I will be assessing your progress throughout. You'll be given a grade at the end of term and the rider with the lowest overall mark will be leaving the class."

Tara's lesson today was a re-introduction to the basics of cross-country. She had set up a short course of just five fences: a small rustic log to begin with and then a low bank that the horse had to drop down, followed by a more substantial bounce fence, then a brush, followed three strides later by a bullfinch – a trimmed hedge that had spindly bits of tree sticking up out of the top of it.

Tara asked the riders to dismount and they walked the stridings on the course while she talked to them about the correct approach for each jump.

"The first jump is straightforward. Consider it a lesson in being focused on what lies ahead," she explained.

"Once you are in mid-air over the log you should already be preparing for the next jump. There are only four strides before you reach the bank, and you'll need to bring your horse back to a trot so they have a chance to get a good look before they jump down."

Tara leapt down the bank and the riders followed her on to the bounce fence.

"Take it at a steady canter. If your horse tries to put in an extra stride, you'll end up in trouble."

Georgie thought that the fourth fence, the brush, would be the toughest. It was almost a metre and a half wide and seemed huge.

"The hedge is the simplest jump," Tara said dismissively. "It's what we call a 'rider frightener'. It might look big and imposing to you, but your horse will take it easily – as long as you don't lose your nerve."

She walked on, measuring out the two strides to the bullfinch. "Don't let your horse hesitate. Otherwise they will balloon over the very tips of the hedge and do an enormous jump rather than staying low through the spindly upper branches as they are supposed to."

The riders remounted and under Tara's watchful eye

they took the course one at a time. Nicholas Laurent went first on his Selle Francais gelding, Lagerfeld, and the others all watched as he flew the first four fences expertly, doing everything by the book. At fence five, however, he forgot what Tara had said and allowed his horse to stand off and do an enormous stag leap that almost unseated him.

"That's OK." Tara wasn't fazed. "Not bad for a first try. Now you'll know to have a bit more impulsion the next time you come at it."

Cameron came through second on Paddy. He took the log fence and then let Paddy charge at the bank.

"Slow to a trot!" Tara shouted. Cameron managed to slow Paddy a little, but the big piebald still took the bank with a flying leap. He took the bounce and the brush beautifully after that and flew the bullfinch perfectly.

"Seat of the pants stuff at the beginning there, Mr Fraser," Tara said. "A bit more control, please! Can we have you now, please, Arden?"

Georgie had really been hoping that Arden and Kennedy might have decided to change classes this term and take a different subject, so she'd been sorely disappointed when she saw the two showjumperettes tacking up that afternoon.

Arden came in at the first jump on her brown mare, Prada, growling at the horse and threatening her with her whip. Prada took a late stride and Arden gave a shriek as she flung her arms around the mare's neck. It looked like she might fall at the first jump, but Arden managed to get back into the saddle and keep going. After that, Prada stumbled her way around to finish the course.

"You need to ride more positively, Miss Mortimer!" Tara told her. "Can we have you next, Georgie?"

All this time, Georgie had been working Belle on a twenty-metre circle. The mare was explosive and kept surging forward with every stride, and Georgie was having trouble calming her down. Tara watched her efforts with concern.

"Did you get a chance to ride her over the mid-term break?"

Georgie shook her head.

Tara nodded. "Well it shows. Five days without being ridden is too much. I suggest you get down to the stables early in the morning and give her some work on a lunge rein before class. She's far too fresh."

Georgie had been so preoccupied with James that she hadn't even thought of lungeing Belle to get rid of her excess energy. Now she realised Tara was right. The horse beneath her was dangerously keen and she was about to tackle a cross-country course.

Things started to go wrong well before they even reached the first jump. Belle began doing little pig roots. These weren't what you'd call a proper buck; Belle's jerky movements were little sproinky leaps of excitement, like a fawn bouncing up in the air on all fours from the sheer joy of being alive.

"Don't try and approach the fence when she's being like that. Give her another circle to settle her in," Tara said with a worried expression on her face.

But Belle didn't settle. As she came in to face the jump she had her nose so far up in the air that she almost smacked Georgie in the face. And as soon as she came down after the log she surged off in such a mad rush that Georgie had no hope of turning her to take the bank. In fact, she had trouble just pulling the mare to a stop.

"You need to react faster when she does that, Miss Parker!" Tara instructed. "Come in over the log again and turn her in time to take the bank."

Georgie did as she was told, but in attempting to steady the mare down to a reasonable speed she hung on to Belle's mouth so tightly that the mare refused point blank to jump the log. Georgie came in to try again, but the mare still refused.

"Stop hanging on." Tara was firm this time. "Let her go."

As they came into the jump, Georgie could feel herself panicking and she threw the reins at Belle right in front of the rustic log. Belle propped and then lunged forward and did a bizarre stag leap sideways over the corner of the fence. Completely taken by surprise, Georgie flew forward in the saddle, losing her stirrups. Unbalanced by her rider, Belle threw in a big buck for good measure and Georgie flew straight up and out of the saddle. She saw the ground coming towards her face in a sickening rush and managed to curl herself up into a ball just in time. The wind got knocked out of her on impact and Georgie felt that awful sensation of being unable to get any air back into her lungs as she gasped like a fish on the ground.

Tara was the first one by her side.

"Stay still," she told Georgie. "Don't hurry to get up – take your time and breathe. Is anything broken?"

Nothing was broken – but Georgie was trembling as she took Belle's reins back from Tara.

"Pop her over the log so she knows she can't get away with refusing it, and then you're done for the day," Tara told her.

Pop her over the log, Georgie thought as she circled Belle into the fence. *Yeah right, easier said than done.* As she came at the jump in a rush, Georgie could feel her classmates' eyes on her. She wanted to make a nice job of it, but instead, Belle flicked her head, yanking the reins free and charging the log at a mad gallop. It was all Georgie could do to stay on her. But the nightmare lesson was over – for Georgie at least. For some students, however, it was just beginning.

"Mitty!" Tara called out, "can you come through now, please?"

Standing beside the jump, Mitty Janssen had been

watching as Georgie and Belle made a hash of the course. She looked very nervous. And now, as she came in to ride at the very first jump, it was clear from Mitty's approach that she was scared.

"Miss Janssen!" Tara called out to her. "Sit up and ride positively into the fence!"

Mitty circled again and came back at the jump at a canter, but way before she had even got close, her big brown Warmblood was swerving and refusing.

"Come in at a strong canter. Sit up and drive him with your legs. Look over the fence and give with your hands!" Tara was calling out instructions, but as Mitty's horse slid to a stop right in front of the jump on the third try it was clearly no use.

"Miss Janssen—" Tara began, but Mitty cut her off.

"No!" she shouted, turning back to face Tara. "You can stop giving me advice. I don't want to do it and the horse doesn't want to do it."

"Mitty, if you'll just…" Tara began again. But Mitty was having none of it. She'd ripped off her back protector and thrown it on the ground at Tara's feet.

"I thought it would be easier this term," she said, tears

welling in her eyes. "But every time it is the same. 'Feel the fear and learn to conquer it.' Well, I am tired of feeling fear. I am a dressage rider. I don't know what I'm even doing in this class!"

She looked at the back protector lying in the mud. "You can give that to someone who needs it," she told Tara. "Because I quit!"

"Well, that was a fun way to kick off this half-term," Alice said as they walked the horses back to the stables. "Poor Mitty – out before we even began."

"I don't blame her. That was the worst class ever," Georgie groaned. "Me and Belle must be bottom of the class ranking after that!"

Alice frowned. "Now Mitty's quit do we still have to worry about elimination?"

"I guess so," Georgie said. "It's not like Tara got rid of her. She got rid of herself."

When they got to the stables, Alice untacked Will and put him in his loose box with his feed while Georgie rugged up Belle.

Even though it had been horrible on the cross-country course, now that she was back in the stables with the mare, Georgie couldn't possibly be angry with her. Belle hadn't meant to do anything naughty – she was just high-spirited and too fresh.

"I know, girl," Georgie said softly as the mare rubbed her muzzle up against her. "I've missed you too. It wasn't your fault out there today."

She led Belle back out to the paddocks with Alice at her side.

"Maybe Belle's getting hot from too much hard feed," Alice offered.

Georgie shook her head. "Tara was right, I should never have just left her for so long without work."

All the same, Georgie decided to cut back on Belle's hard feed in future. She let Belle go and stood at the gate with Alice and watched as the mare strolled over to the muddiest spot in the paddock, dropped down on her knees and had a vigorous roll, grunting with pleasure as her legs thrashed in the air. When she stood up and shook out her mane, clumps of turf went flying in every direction.

Georgie groaned. "Look at her! She's filthy! It's going to take me forever to get her clean again."

"Poor Georgie," Alice said. "It really hasn't been your day, has it?"

They were heading back through the stable towards the boarding houses when Georgie said, "Wait a minute, I just need to put my halter away."

She made a detour to the tack room and was about to turn the handle on the door when she heard voices. There was murmuring and giggling on the other side of the tack-room door. She could hear a girl and a boy whispering to each other. Georgie froze for a second and was about to turn away when the door opened and there was Arden Mortimer standing right in front of her!

Arden's face was flushed and her long dark hair was loose over her shoulders. When she saw Georgie her smile dropped for a moment, then she gave a smug smirk and said, "Oh, well, I guess you had to find out sooner or later."

Arden pushed past and left Georgie standing there, staring at the boy with whom she had obviously just been snogging. Georgie couldn't believe it. And yet in a way she already knew it would be him. She took one last look at James Kirkwood, then turned and ran, before he had the chance to see her cry.

Chapter Seven

When Georgie had found Arden and James in the garden together that night at the Kirkwood mansion, she believed him when he said it was perfectly innocent. Now she was reconsidering. Had it started back then? Was that why James had abandoned her? It was so embarrassing to think that the Burghley House boys and the showjumperettes all knew about this before she did. It was bad enough being dumped – but being tossed aside for a superficial showjumperette like Arden Mortimer really sucked.

Luckily for Georgie, her failed love life was about to be eclipsed by a much more outrageous scandal. The appointment of Hans Schockelmann as the showjumping coach at Adelaide House had the whole school talking, and not in a good way. Georgie had heard the rumours, but it wasn't until the showjumping team meeting at Badminton House that she got the full story from a furious Kendal Dupree.

"It's cheating – straight out dirty cheating!" Kendal said. "Hans is ranked the number one showjumper in the world! They can't have him as team coach. It's like getting Stephen Hawking to help you with your science homework!"

Georgie was confused. "Why don't Adelaide just have one of the house masters like the other teams do?"

"They say it's a 'loophole'," Kendal did sarcastic air quotes. "Apparently if the regular coach isn't available then the teams can find their own. Adelaide House were supposed to have Miss Loden, but she's away so they roped in Hans Schockelmann as her replacement!"

Georgie still didn't understand. "If he's the best showjumper in the world then how come he's willing to coach Adelaide House?"

"Two words," Kendal said. "Patricia Kirkwood. Patricia has been employing Hans to give Kennedy private jumping lessons for ages. Apparently she offered to sponsor his horses for the next Olympics if he agreed to coach the team."

Apart from Hans Schockelmann at Adelaide, all the other boarding houses had Blainford masters as team coaches. Burghley House had Heath Brompton, the polo master, and Trent Chase, head of the showjumping department, was coaching Luhmuhlen. Georgie wasn't sure if it was a stroke of luck or just the opposite that Badminton House had been handed to Tara Kelly.

"OK, she'll probably work us like dogs, but at least Tara knows how to jump," Alice insisted. "It's Stars of Pau I feel sorry for. Imagine being lumbered with Ms Schmidt!"

Bettina Schmidt was strictly a dressage rider and didn't know a coloured pole from a cavaletti. In fact it was a toss-up between Stars of Pau and Lexington House as to who came off worst. Lexington had Hank Shepard, the head of the Western faculty.

"Great!" Daisy King said sarcastically. "What's he gonna do? Lasso the jumps and hog-tie them?"

Of the six squad members gathered on the sofa in the Badminton House main common room, Georgie already knew three: Alice, Daisy and Kendal. The other two riders were Amy Davis and Karen Lockhart. The girls were both juniors – a term which actually meant they were in their third year at the Academy. Amy was a showjumping major, a pixie-like girl with short-cropped brown hair. She rode a chestnut Hanoverian with the fancy show name Sandhurst Debonair – although his paddock-name was Sandy. Karen Lockhart was a showjumper as well. Her horse was nicknamed Rocky – short for Rolling Rock – a big, dark brown mare with a white blaze and three white socks.

Georgie had seen Karen and Amy around the house before, although the juniors seldom hung out with first years and had their own common room on the upper floor of the boarding house. For today's meeting, they had gathered downstairs and Kendal had produced a packet of chocolate biscuits, which were normally under lock and key, and reserved for guests alone. The girls had eaten half the packet by the time Tara Kelly arrived and the meeting began.

Tara was straight down to business. "The tournament

is in two stages," she told the girls. "The first of these is the sudden-death knockout in three weeks' time. There are six teams – one from each house. The three houses that win in the knockouts continue through to the finals, so this round is crucial. If we don't win then we're out."

Tara's training schedule was rigorous. "The squad meets on Mondays and Wednesdays after school, and on Saturday mornings at seven for the next three weeks," she told the girls.

There was a groan from some of the squad members.

"Fine," Tara said. "We'll make it six-thirty instead, shall we?" She reached over and took the half-eaten packet of chocolate biscuits that Kendal had been hiding under the table.

"And no more junk food! Your horses are on a fitness regime and you should be too. Drop the chocolate biscuits and get yourselves to the gym. I want this team in top shape."

The girls cast a longing look at the biscuits as Tara shoved them in her bag.

"This team has the talent to win the House Cup and I plan to make sure that we do," Tara said. Georgie heard a tetchy note in Tara's voice as she added, "There's no way I'm going to lose to Hans Schockelmann!"

"Tara absolutely hates Hans," Alice said as they walked to their cross-country lesson the next Monday. "They used to date back when she was at Blainford and he dumped her just before the School Formal."

"That's so cruel!" Georgie was shocked.

"Apparently she never spoke to him again," Alice said.

"I'm so sick of hearing about the School Formal," Daisy said dismissively. "Why does everyone keep talking about it? Does it earn us points for the class ranking?"

"No, Daisy." Alice looked at her like she was from Mars. "It's for fun."

Daisy wrinkled her nose up. "Yeah, whatever."

"It's not fun so far," Emily groaned. "It's torture. The other day Alex came over at lunch and I thought he was finally going to ask me, but then he just said, 'Are you going to eat your pudding or can I have it?'"

"Well, if you want to go with him, why don't you ask him?" Alice said.

"Yeah, well, why don't you ask Cameron?" Emily countered.

Alice turned bright pink. All the girls in Badminton House suspected that Alice had a crush on Cam, but she would never admit it.

"So, let me get this straight," Georgie said. "None of us have dates for the Formal?"

The other girls nodded glumly.

"After your performance last week," Daisy said. "I'd spend more time worrying about cross-country elimination Georgie, if I were you."

"Daisy!" Alice said.

"What?" Daisy frowned. "Oh, come on! Georgie knows it's true – she's at the bottom of the class."

Daisy was brutally honest and dead right. Georgie had to raise her game if she wanted to be in Tara's class beyond the end of term.

"We're going to take the horses out to the steeplechase section of the course today," Tara told them. "The jumps are not big, and they're not complex. This is all about getting the horses working at a nice, regular gallop through the course."

The steeplechase was the same course they had ridden for their mid-term exam, a series of low natural fences like spars and hedges that could be taken at a fair speed. As Georgie headed over to the start of the course, she recognised the wiry, hunched figure of the school's caretaker, Kenny, moving jump stands from the arena to the equipment shed nearby.

Kenny did odd jobs around the Academy and was the school's driver. When Georgie had first arrived in Lexington it had been Kenny who had met her at the airport to drive her to Blainford, and although Georgie sometimes had trouble understanding his Kentucky drawl and was a bit grossed out by his habit of mulching his chewing tobacco around in his mouth as he spoke, she really liked him.

"Hi, Kenny!" Georgie called out.

"Georgie!" Kenny grinned at her and put down the jump stand he was carrying to come over and say hello. "Hey, how's that mare of yours goin'?"

"We got into the House Showjumping team," Georgie said proudly.

"Good for you!" Kenny said.

It's funny, Georgie thought, *even when he's talking to you, he always has at least one eye on your horse.* As they chatted, she could see he was watching the way Belle was behaving, crab-stepping beneath Georgie, incapable of standing still.

"She's restless, ain't she?" Kenny said. "She always like this when you're on the course?"

"She was too fresh last week," Georgie admitted, "but I've given her loads of work since then. She'll be totally different this time."

Kenny didn't look convinced. "A lot of Thoroughbred in her," he observed. "She's got the build – and the temperament too. A hot-head. Got your hands full with this mare, that's for sure." He paused to spit out his chewing tobacco. "I got a nephew, he's a jockey. Rides trackwork at Clemency Farm, out past Pleasant Hill," Kenny said. "Riley Conway's his name. That boy has a way with horses I've never seen before. If one of the other jockeys has a horse they can't make headway with, they send 'em to Riley. There ain't a horse that boy can't figure out. He'd be able to help with this mare, for sure."

"Thanks, Kenny," Georgie said, feeling slightly resentful to be given advice when her horse hadn't even done anything wrong yet. "But Belle isn't a racehorse. She doesn't need to learn how to go around a track."

"You know what my dad always used to say?" Kenny smiled. "He'd say a horse is a horse is a horse."

Georgie pulled a face. "Uh, that's not much of a 'saying', Kenny."

The caretaker shook his head. "My dad wasn't no poet. But he knew his horses. And he was right. Don't matter whether you want to race 'em or jump 'em or just ride 'em around the arena doing fancy-pants dressage. It's all the same inside their heads; that horse is still a horse. You gotta think like they do. That's what Riley does. He thinks like a horse."

Kenny put his hand up to stroke Belle on the muzzle. "He's a good boy, Riley. Happy to help you any time. It's not far to Clemency Farm – I can give you his phone number. Maybe you can take the mare over to see him?"

Georgie smiled. "Thanks, Kenny, but Belle is going to be fine today. She just had too much energy last week, that's all. You'll see."

Kenny nodded. "Maybe that's true like you say, Georgie. I hope so."

By the time Georgie caught up with the other riders, Tara Kelly was explaining how she wanted them to ride the steeplechase course.

"Learning how to maintain a steady gallop on the cross-country course is vital, to conserve your horse's energy. Today I want you to allow them to relax into a rhythm all the way round – no speeding!"

On the start line, Georgie looked at her classmates, thinking back to their mid-term exam. She'd learned a few lessons that day – the main one being not to ride anywhere near Kennedy or Daisy. Kennedy had actually pushed Georgie off on purpose during the exam. And

Daisy? Georgie's British rival didn't mean to be dangerous, but she was ruthlessly competitive. She had a habit of barging through to the front of the pack and running over anyone who got in her way.

Georgie had positioned herself at the far side of the field, next to Cameron and Alex. Belle was only too aware that they were about to ride the point-to-point course and was skipping and dancing, going up on her hindquarters then lunging suddenly forward, trying to get Georgie to release the reins.

"Steady, Belle," Georgie whispered to the mare. "Not much longer…"

When Tara finally called out, "On your marks… go!" Belle shot forward like a rocket, but Georgie was ready for her. She'd remembered some of Kenny's advice from the last time she'd raced and wrapped her hands in Belle's mane. It stopped her from being left behind in the saddle as the mare lurched forward and broke into a gallop.

"Steady, girl!" Georgie immediately gave a tug on the reins to get Belle back under control. She was taken by surprise when the mare gave a defiant flick of her head and pulled the reins clean out of Georgie's hands.

"Belle!" Georgie managed to gather up the reins again and set her whole bodyweight against the mare, but it was no good. Belle was far too strong and she wasn't listening. She was flat out in full gallop and didn't slow down even slightly as she took the first fence, barging past Alex and Nicholas.

A few strides out from the next fence Georgie sat back in the saddle, pulling both reins as hard as she could. This time Belle flung her head in the air, nearly striking Georgie in the face with her poll. This was a nightmare! The more Georgie tried to slow Belle down, the more the mare defied her and flew at the fences. They took the jump at a blind gallop, Belle landed badly and nearly fell on the other side of the fence. Georgie managed to pull Belle's head up to stop the mare from stumbling to her knees, but the shock of near-disaster made her realise the horrifying truth. She had absolutely no control whatsoever – Belle was bolting and Georgie couldn't stop her.

At the fourth jump, the moment Belle felt the pressure

of the bit in her mouth she resisted. The battle between her and Georgie made the mare go even wilder. They'd passed Emily Tait back at the last fence and were in the lead, but that had never been Georgie's intention. This was supposed to be a slow, steady exercise, a display of the rider's control of their horse. But Belle was the one in charge, and Georgie was helpless.

Over the next four fences, Belle never slowed down and Georgie felt as if her arms were about to be ripped out of their sockets. As they flew the final jump, Georgie was amazed that she was still on Belle's back. It took her another half a kilometre to pull the mare up and by the time she came back to rejoin the others she was as white as a sheet and shaking. Tara looked worried.

"I'm fine," Georgie insisted. But as she dismounted she felt her legs give way beneath her and Tara only just managed to grab her as Georgie collapsed on the ground.

"Put your head between your knees and take deep breaths," Tara said as she crouched beside her.

"I tried to hold her, but she just kept fighting," Georgie told Tara, her words trembly. "I don't know why she's like this on the cross-country. She was brilliant in the showjumping arena…"

Georgie took another deep breath and fought back the tears. She knew it sounded pathetic, but it was true. Belle had been fine in the showjumping. She'd been OK in Bettina's dressage class last week as well. Why was it that in the only class that really mattered to Georgie, the mare always turned into a basket-case?

"I've seen a lot of horses that were as cool as a cucumber in the show ring and became headstrong on the cross-country," Tara said. "It looks like Belle might be one of them."

Tara looked over at Belle. The mare was drenched in sweat and heaving with the exertion of her mad gallop. "You'd better rug her up and walk her or she'll get a chill."

Georgie pulled herself up and did as Tara said. She took Belle, rugged her up and walked the mare to cool her down before grooming her, feeding her and turning her out. When she returned to the stables to hang up her halter she found Tara waiting for her.

"Georgie," Tara said, "I think we need to talk."

She followed Tara through the stables to the tack room and sat down while Tara made them both a cup of tea. She had been here once before with her teacher and that time they'd talked about Georgie's mum. Tara had been at school with Ginny Parker and although the two of them had been rivals, they'd also been friends. Tara had a soft spot for Georgie because of this. Or at least so Georgie thought.

"You realise that you're coming bottom of the class, don't you?" Tara began straight away.

Georgie didn't know what to say. "We've had a couple of bad weeks," she responded meekly, "I'm trying…"

"Georgie, I didn't bring you in here to give you a telling-off," Tara sighed. "I can't play favourites and give you extra tuition, but I do think you need someone to help you with Belle."

"Belle is fine – she's just fresh, she'll change…" Georgie protested stubbornly. But Tara shook her head.

"When I was competing, a lot of my horses were very hot like Belle," Tara said. "You can't expect them to miraculously alter their character. You have to change. It's up to you to learn to let her go." Tara looked serious.

"This horse will be the making of you, Georgie. For every rider, there is one horse that elevates them to a new level. Belle can do that for you – if you let her. But you need to find a way forward with this mare because right now you're in danger of failing my class. If you don't get the grades this half-term, then I'll have no choice but to eliminate you."

The walk down the driveway back to Badminton House seemed to take forever that evening. Georgie's boots felt like they had lead in them. There was no one else in the boarding house – the others must have already headed up to the dining hall for dinner – but Georgie didn't mind being left behind; she wasn't hungry anyway.

Exhausted, she headed straight for her dorm room, and that was when she saw the envelope pinned to the outside of her door. Inside there was a card with a handwritten message – just a phone number and a name. Georgie looked at it for a moment and then took the card into the lobby of the boarding house, picked up the phone and dialled the number. The phone rang and rang, then, just as Georgie was about to hang up, someone answered.

"Hello," the voice at the other end of the line said, "this is Riley Conway."

Chapter Eight

When Riley Conway gave Georgie directions to Clemency Farm he made them sound easy. Look for a white fence and a beaten-up green letterbox, turn down the driveway and ride until you reach a barn with a green roof. But this was bluegrass country, home to over five hundred horse farms, the green fields went on forever, their white plank fencelines merging into one another. Georgie had been riding for almost half an hour now and everything looked the same! It was impossible to tell where one farm finished and the next one began.

She was just beginning to despair when she caught sight of a pale green letterbox, the metal all crumpled like a paper bag. She turned down the driveway and in the distance she could make out a barn with a green roof. This must be the place.

As she walked Belle down the driveway, two Thoroughbred yearlings, a chestnut and a bay, craned their necks over the paddock rails to whinny hellos and then began trotting back and forth along the fenceline, their heads held high, their eyes fixed on the visitors. Surprised by their attentions, Belle boggled and snorted.

"It's OK, girl." Georgie gave the mare a reassuring pat on the neck. "They're just being friendly."

The yearlings kept pace companionably on the other side of the fence all the way to the end of the driveway. Their nickers echoed around the empty stable yard, announcing Georgie's arrival.

"Hello?" Georgie dismounted and ran Belle's stirrups up, leading the mare alongside, her horseshoes chiming out against the concrete surface of the yard. She'd expected Clemency Farm to be like all the other horse farms around here with their glamorous stables and flashy facilities. Instead, this yard wasn't much more than a wash bay, a couple of pens and a hitching rail.

"Is anyone here?" Georgie called out. There was still

no reply so she led Belle into the barn. It was a dark space, with a high curved ceiling and concrete floors. There were no fancy loose boxes, but there were four wooden railed pens with fresh straw laid out on the floor. Three of these pens contained young racehorses: two chestnuts and a steel grey colt. At the sight of Belle, they raised their heads.

"Riley?" Georgie called out. She was beginning to think that maybe he'd forgotten she was coming. She walked all the way through the barn to the back doors that had been slid wide open to let in the morning sunlight. Behind the barn, there was a small, round pen and beyond that, a large field bordered by a racetrack.

Georgie heard the sound of hoofbeats before she caught sight of the horse and rider. They were galloping at the far end of the track. The rider was perched jockey-style; his stirrups so short that his knees were tucked up underneath him, his body bent over the horse's withers. The jockey held a whip in his hand, but he didn't appear to be using it. In fact he hardly seemed to move at all as the horse strode out beneath him, swallowing the ground with magnificent ease. They were taking the corner and heading back for home, in full gallop as they flew out around the bend of the track towards the barn.

As the horse drew closer, Georgie could see that it was big, maybe seventeen hands high, solidly built and jet black with no white markings, galloping with a natural ease that only true Thoroughbreds possess.

They headed into the home stretch, and the jockey lifted the whip. He held it in the air near the horse's face as if he was showing it to the big, black Thoroughbred. The horse seemed to understand his meaning and his strides came even faster. He stretched out long and low, increasing speed as they bore down on the finish line. Georgie could see the strain showing in every inch of the animal's body, the muscles rippling beneath the shiny black coat, the white foam of sweat beginning to appear on the horse's neck. As the jockey galloped past an orange marker post beside the track, he reached for the stopwatch on his wrist.

It took another hundred metres for the horse to ease up. The jockey stood quietly in his stirrups, steadying back to a canter, then a trot and finally a walk as he headed back towards Georgie.

"You Georgie Parker?" he called out to her.

Georgie nodded.

"Get on your horse and come out and join me," the jockey said.

Georgie was a bit surprised by this request. But she did as he said, mounting up and riding Belle out on to the track.

The jockey shoved his whip down the side of his boot for safekeeping while he yanked off his helmet and mud-splattered racing goggles. He raked a hand through his damp, dark brown hair.

"Sorry," he said to Georgie. "I thought I'd be finished by the time you turned up. Do you mind walking along the track for a while so I can cool Talisman down?"

Georgie stared at the jockey. Now that he had taken off his helmet and track goggles she could see that he had green eyes, wide cheekbones and a nose that might have been broken once and had mended slightly crooked, giving him an off-kilter look that didn't destroy his handsomeness so much as enhance it. But that wasn't holding Georgie's attention. It was his age, or rather, lack of it. She'd been expecting to meet an adult, a professional.

But the jockey on the black horse couldn't have been more than fifteen. He was a teenager, just like her!

"I thought you'd be old!" Georgie blurted out without thinking.

Riley smiled. "Nope," he said. "I'm pretty sure I'm not."

He turned the black horse around on the track and began to walk. "You'll have to keep up with me," he said. "I really need to give Talisman a cool-down."

He looked over his shoulder at Georgie, who hadn't moved.

"You coming?"

What else could Georgie do? It had taken an hour to get here. She might as well give him five more minutes – even though she failed to see how he could teach her anything about horses that she didn't already know.

"So," Riley said, "this is the mare that you've been having trouble with?"

Georgie didn't have to answer. Belle, who had been crab-stepping anxiously along the race track as if her hooves were touching hot sand, suddenly went up in a half-rear and then tried to bolt. Georgie had to twist her around in a tight circle, reacting like lightning to stop the mare from taking off.

Riley watched this performance and then looked questioningly at Georgie. "Do you always ride her like that?" he asked.

Georgie was puzzled. "Like what?"

"Hangin' on to the reins."

"You saw what she just did!" Georgie said. "If I don't hang on she'll bolt."

Riley looked unconvinced. "If you keep holding on like that then pretty soon that mare will be thinking backwards. If I were you I'd—"

Georgie snapped. "Listen, Mr Horse Whisperer. You can lay off, OK? I know how to ride. I'm a student at Blainford Academy. I won the UK auditions!"

Riley looked nonplussed by Georgie's outburst. "The UK? I thought you were from England?"

"It's the same thing!" Georgie completely lost the plot now. "And it's beside the point."

"First of all," Riley said, "I think you need to calm down. I can see that you're a pretty good rider. But I can also see that this mare doesn't like to be held back, and

I'm pretty sure that most of your problems are a battle of wills between you two."

He smiled at Georgie. "You like to win your battles. Trouble is, this mare is just the same as you, so you keep fighting. You need to come up with a new plan. Out-think her. Do the opposite – stop hanging on and let her go."

"Unbelievable!" Georgie scowled at the boy. "You've only just met me and Belle and already you think you can psychoanalyse our relationship?"

"Why don't you listen to what I have to say about this mare and then decide," Riley replied.

"OK, Mr Horse Whisperer," Georgie said, "go ahead – tell me all about Belle."

Riley looked at Belle and thought hard for a moment before he spoke. "She's half Thoroughbred and half Warmblood," he said, assessing her physique with an expert eye. "She's a great jumper in the show ring, but the minute you get her out on the cross-country course something inside her clicks and she won't listen to you. She gets too strong to hold so you fight her, then she sticks her head in the air, the jumps rush up at you and

124

it ends in disaster. You're starting to get scared of her. You don't trust her enough any more to let her go." He paused. "That boarding school of yours could probably give you another horse, but you don't want to give up on this mare. You still love her, and there's something between you two that goes deeper than it does with most horses and riders." Riley's voice softened. "You ain't ready to give up, not yet anyway, and that's why you're here."

Georgie almost burst into tears. She'd never heard anyone put into words exactly how she felt about riding Belle.

"How... how did you know?" she said.

"Lucky guess," Riley replied. He turned Talisman around. "Come on, I think he's cooled down enough," he told Georgie. "Bring your mare. We'll work in the round pen today. She'll have nowhere to run – except in circles."

The first thing Riley did in the round pen was take away Georgie's reins. "You won't need these," he told her, knotting them and clipping a lunge rein on to the bridle.

Riley made Georgie ride around the round pen, steering and controlling Belle with her legs, putting her hands on her hips, then her shoulders, and her thighs – even behind her back. She thought that Belle would try to bolt without being held, but the mare kept a calm, steady pace.

"That's because you're using your body, voice and legs to control her speed," Riley explained. "This is the first step to break your reliance on the reins," he told Georgie. "Find your balance and power without them and learn not to hold Belle back all the time."

Despite herself, Georgie had to admit that Riley's methods seemed to work. By the end of their session, Belle was moving beautifully and freely and Georgie felt like they had made real progress. She thanked Riley and offered to pay him, but he shook his head. "You're a friend of Uncle Kenny's," he told her. "You don't owe me anything."

An hour without any reins was hard work and Georgie felt exhausted. She could hardly face the thought of the hour-long ride back to school.

"I've got soda and some lemon cake my mom made," Riley told her. "Why don't you tie Belle up and have something to eat before you go?"

He led the way into the stables. There was an old, overstuffed sofa at the far end of the barn and beside the sofa, a fridge from which Riley produced the drinks and cake. They sat down next to each other on the sofa.

"So are you here by yourself all week?" Georgie asked.

Riley smiled. "I'm not some hillbilly – I go to school too, you know. I ride in the mornings before class most days. We take the horses for trackwork down at Keeneland Park. My dad manages Clemency Farm and I help him out – he gives me the run of the place on Saturdays so that he can have a day off work."

"Oh," Georgie felt foolish. "I thought it was your yard."

"It will be someday, I suppose," Riley said.

"So what school do you go to?"

"Pleasant Hill High."

"Do you like it?"

"I don't hate it," Riley replied.

"You should try and get into Blainford next year," Georgie said. "They teach all kinds of riding there."

"Yeah, it's on my list of things to do right after buying a super-yacht and a mansion," Riley said.

"Not everyone there is rich," Georgie countered.

"It must be weird – actually living at your school," Riley continued. "Mom says that she feels sorry for kids at boarding school. She says it must be awful having a family who don't love you enough to keep you home with them…"

As soon as the words were out he realised what he'd said. "I'm sorry, Georgie, that came out wrong. I'm sure your parents aren't like that."

"It's OK," Georgie said. "I think my dad kind of felt the same way as your mum, but I really wanted to go to Blainford, so I convinced him."

"What about your mom?" Riley asked.

"She died," Georgie said, "four years ago. She was a professional eventing rider, but she had a bad accident on the cross-country course."

"I'm really sorry," Riley shook his head. "I didn't mean to bring it up."

"That's OK," Georgie said, "I don't talk about her very often. She was my hero, I guess. She's part of the reason

I went to Blainford. I want to be an eventing rider one day, just like her."

"That's what I want too," Riley said.

"I thought you'd want to be a jockey."

"Are you kidding me?" Riley grinned and helped himself to a second slice of the lemon cake. "For starters, I'm already way too tall. Plus, I love to eat. I'm not willing to starve myself to make race-weight. I'm only just light enough now to ride trackwork."

Georgie was hesitant to ask if she could come and have another lesson, but as Riley said goodbye he added, "So I guess I'll see you the same time next weekend?"

"I have showjumping training on Saturday," Georgie said, "but I could come on Sunday."

"See you then," Riley agreed.

He gave Georgie a leg-up on to Belle and she set off towards the gate. At the mailbox she turned to wave goodbye, but Riley had already gone.

Chapter Nine

A storm had been threatening all weekend, but it wasn't until Monday that the rain finally began to fall. Georgie sat in Ms Schmidt's class that morning and watched the raindrops forming tiny rivers down the windowpane.

They were supposed to be conjugating verbs, but Georgie found it hard to focus. She kept thinking back to the weekend, about Clemency Farm and Riley Conway.

Riley was like no one she'd ever met before. "He knew straight away what was wrong with Belle," Georgie told Alice as they left German class and walked around the quad.

"So he's horse psychic?" Alice pulled a face.

"No," Georgie said, "I mean he's really instinctively

talented. You know, here we are studying how to be riders and it just comes naturally to him."

"What does he look like?" asked Alice.

"What's that got to do with anything?" Georgie replied.

"I don't know," Alice grinned. "You just seem pretty into him, that's all."

"Alice!" Georgie laughed. "It's not like that! He's just helping me with Belle."

The weather continued to worsen and got so bad that by the afternoon even Tara Kelly had admitted defeat and their cross-country lesson was cancelled. The fields were too wet and the rain was too heavy, so the students were handed over to Mrs Winton, the grooming mistress, for a practical horsemanship lesson in the stables instead.

Mrs Winton was a stickler for detail. Her grooming lessons were often tedious, as she demanded the students get things absolutely perfect. Georgie once spent an entire week plaiting and unplaiting a Spanish running plait on a piece of rope tied to a post before Mrs Winton was satisfied enough to allow Georgie to progress on to a real mane. She was a robust woman and always wore a tweed hacking jacket and a bowler hat that drew attention to her round face and ruddy, weather-beaten cheeks.

The students arrived to find her oiling a large pair of electric shears and looking like she meant business. "Nicholas," Mrs Winton said, "can you bring Lagerfeld out of his box? I'm going to demonstrate how to do a trace clip."

Nicholas led Lagerfeld to the teacher and held him as she took a piece of white chalk and began to draw a pattern on the horse's body.

"Some people clip without a chalk line, but the end result looks messy," Mrs Winton told them as she sketched a straight line horizontally along Lagerfeld's belly. "You must make the chalk line even on both sides, down the gullet of the neck, along the belly and then a second line at the top of the legs…"

Then Mrs Winton began. She held the clippers against Lagerfeld's neck first, to get him accustomed to the sound. Then, when the horse didn't flinch, she turned the clippers and pressed the blade against his skin. The horses all had thick winter coats and Lagerfeld's fuzz peeled off in long strips as Mrs Winton shaved him. She worked swiftly and confidently, talking constantly as she went, giving tips on how to attack certain bits like the tricky area behind the elbow. Within minutes there was a huge pile of russet-coloured horse fluff all over the concrete floor of the stables and Lagerfeld's neck and belly had been shaved as smooth as a seal.

Mrs Winton moved around the horse to work on the other side. As soon as she was out of sight, Kennedy and Arden began giggling and grabbing handfuls of fluff off the stable floor, throwing it at each other like snowballs.

"Girls!" Mrs Winton stuck her head over Lagerfeld's back and caught Kennedy in mid-throw. "I hope you've been paying attention and not just fooling around, because now it's your turn."

The teacher walked over to a stack of clipper boxes and began to hand them out. "You're going be clipping your own horse."

Kennedy looked horrified. "But Mrs Winton, we get a man in to do our horses!"

"As a professional eventing rider, you will have as many as twelve horses in work," Mrs Winton replied.

"You'll save a fortune if you can do this yourself."

"I don't care about the money," Kennedy sniffed.

Mrs Winton thrust a clipper box into her hands. "Think of it as a beauty parlour for ponies," she suggested. "You can give them a manicure afterwards if you want."

Mrs Winton made her way around the rest of the class. "You'll have to share the clippers," she said, "so split yourselves into groups of three."

Georgie was sharing with Alice and Cameron, and while Alice went to get Will from his stall, Georgie began to examine the illustrations that Mrs Winton had stuck to the wall, showing them the various types of clip to choose from.

"I'm going to do an Irish Clip on Belle," Georgie said when Alice returned.

Alice looked around. "Where's Cameron?"

"I thought he was with you," replied Georgie.

They finally found him with the showjumperettes. Kennedy had managed to get her clippers jammed before they'd even started.

"I nearly broke a nail," she was telling Cameron as she held up her perfectly painted violet nails for his inspection.

She smiled sweetly, looking up through her long eyelashes as she handed him the clippers. "I think these need a man's touch. Can you get them working for me?"

"Sure," Cameron said. He tried the clasp on the handset, but it wouldn't budge. He began grunting and straining, trying to work it loose.

"Ughhh!" His face turned pink with exertion. "They're stuck!"

Alice couldn't stand watching this for a moment longer. She stomped over and grabbed the clippers off Cameron and in one deft move flipped the clasp open. "You had the safety catch on," she told him.

"I knew that," Cameron muttered.

"Well, if you're quite finished flirting with the showjumperettes," Alice said snidely, "we could actually use you back on your own team."

Cameron turned even pinker. "Sorry, Kennedy," he said. "Gotta go."

"Later," Kennedy purred.

"Oh, good grief." Alice rolled her eyes as she walked back to William, waiting patiently for his chalk line to be drawn on.

Georgie held William steady so Alice could draw an outline and then clip him. Cameron, however, was no help at all and kept gazing over at Kennedy.

When Alice had finished, the girls stood back to admire his hunter clip. Will was shaved all over except for his legs and a saddle shape on his back. There were a few stray tufts and it was a little uneven, but not a bad effort.

"Come on," Georgie looked at her watch. "We've got two more horses to do and it's already three o'clock."

With time running short, the girls chalked Paddy and then left Cameron to do the clipping on his own while they brought Belladonna in from the field.

"Did you see?" Alice asked as they led Belle to the stables. "The way Cam keeps drooling over Kennedy?"

Georgie couldn't help noticing it. And she could see how much it upset Alice too. Ever since the very first day at Blainford, Cameron had been embarrassingly fixated on Kennedy Kirkwood. Georgie didn't blame him. With her glossy blow-dried hair and lean, tanned limbs, Kennedy was kind of gorgeous. Like all the showjumperettes, she ignored the uniform rules and wore jewellery and make-up every day. While the other girls wore regulation knee-length skirts, Kennedy and Arden and Tori had theirs altered so they finished halfway up their thighs. Even Kennedy's navy jodhpurs weren't the usual school regulation version – they were tight-fitting, expensive Pikeur jods that her stepmother brought back for her from Paris. *Face it*, Georgie thought, *what boy wouldn't fancy Kennedy Kirkwood*?

They were walking back into the stables and Alice was still moaning about Cameron when Georgie looked at Paddy and let out a shriek of horror. "Ohmygod! Cam, stop!"

Cameron couldn't hear her shouts. The noise of the clippers drowned them out. Georgie raced forward and grabbed them from his hands.

"Hey! What did you do that for?" Cam was shocked.

"Look at what you've done to him!" Georgie pointed at the piebald gelding.

Poor, poor Paddy. Cameron had been so busy gawping at Kennedy that he'd barely been paying attention when the girls drew the chalk line on the black and white horse. When Cameron had started to clip Paddy he was so distracted that he had lost track of the chalk line and instead he'd begun to follow the white markings on the piebald by mistake. Instead of doing a neat straight line across Paddy's tummy he'd veered off and begun to shave the outline of the white patches instead. He'd shaved off all the white bits on Paddy's belly! Cameron's horse looked like a half-finished jigsaw puzzle.

"Mr Fraser." Mrs Winton was stunned. "This is the worst clip I have ever seen! What were you thinking?"

She took the clippers roughly out of Cameron's hands. "Give me those. You're a menace."

Everyone thought the jigsaw clip was hilarious, except for Cam. His mistake had lowered his position in the class ranking – plus it would take two months at least for Paddy's patchwork coat to grow back.

The weather had cleared enough for showjumping training to go ahead that evening after class so Georgie, Alice and Daisy took their freshly clipped horses down to the showjumping arena along with Amy, Kendal and Karen.

Tara was in the arena setting up jumps when they arrived. "We're going to begin with some gridwork," she told them. "I want you to come through over the canter poles and then push your horses on so that they do two big strides between the cross rails."

The girls had only just begun warming up when Conrad Miller appeared with Damien Danforth, Andrew Hurley, Nicholas Laurent and James Kirkwood.

Georgie stiffened at the sight of James. "What are they doing here?" Alice muttered. Tara was wondering the same thing. "Sorry, boys," she told them. "You'll have to ride somewhere else. We're in the middle of a training session."

"So are we," Conrad replied. "Burghley House has booked this arena for showjumping."

Following the boys into the arena was Heath Brompton, the polo master at Blainford. He was also Burghley's house master and coach for the showjumping competition.

"Sorry, Tara," he said. "There appears to be a double booking. Would you mind sharing the arena?"

"I guess we don't really have a choice," Tara sighed.

She began to dismantle her grid of jumps. "We'll use one end of the arena and you use the other."

Georgie held on to Kendal and Amy's reins while the girls went to help Tara construct a new jumping course at one end of the arena.

Meanwhile, James, Andrew and Nicholas helped their coach do likewise at the other end, leaving Damien and Conrad holding on to their horses.

Damien led the horses over so that he could talk to Georgie. "So," he said, "you made the team?"

Georgie nodded. "You too."

There was an awkward silence and then Damien said, "Listen, James will never admit it, but I know he still cares about you. He wants to talk to you, but that idiot Conrad keeps giving him a hard time."

"I wish he would talk to me," Georgie said. "That's all I want."

"I know," Damien nodded, "but he's still hurt, you know – after what you did."

He saw the look of astonishment on Georgie's face. "Hey," Damien added hastily, "I'm not blaming you, I'm just saying—"

He looked over his shoulder. "I'd better go. Can't spend this long talking to the enemy, can I?"

He turned the horses around and walked back towards Conrad, who called out in a booming voice. "Oi, seagull!"

Conrad glared over at them and as Damien rejoined the group Georgie watched as Andrew Hurley began taunting him, flapping his arms and cawing like a gull.

"What are they doing?" Georgie was baffled.

Alice rolled her eyes. "It's this stupid tradition at Burghley House. They do it if they catch one of their members hanging out with anyone that Conrad deems uncool."

Georgie knew she definitely qualified. "But why 'seagull'?"

Alice groaned. "Because only a seagull hangs out with the garbage. Lame, huh?"

For the rest of the training session, Georgie tried to ignore the Burghley boys, but she couldn't help thinking about what Damien had said. What was that stuff about blaming her? It was James who'd taken off without any explanation!

Even though she hated herself for it, she still thought about him all too often. She had daydreams that he would suddenly have a change of heart and confess that it had all been a terrible mistake.

Being here with James in the arena, Georgie had worried that she was going to wig out and get so self-conscious that she wouldn't be able to ride. But Conrad's taunting actually helped her to find some steel inside herself and harden up. Conrad and the polo boys thought she wasn't good enough, huh? They weren't good enough!

As she rode Belle through the gridwork she'd never felt so focused, so competitive. And it showed. If Tara asked them to jump a combination with a single stride they could do it. If she asked Georgie to hold the mare back and put in three little strides instead, well, Georgie could manage that too. As they kept working on their stridings, Tara kept on raising the rails and by the time they had finished their training session, Georgie and Belle were easily clearing a metre thirty – the height that would be required for the first knockout round of the showjumping competition in just over a week's time.

The rest of the riders all performed well too, and Tara seemed genuinely happy with her team.

"That was nice, solid work today," she told them as they left the arena. "If we can build on this level of performance then we've got an excellent chance of making it through to the finals."

"Do we know who we're competing against in the first round yet?" Alice asked.

"No," Tara said. "But I should have the team draw soon."

As Tara was talking, Georgie was watching Arden Mortimer, who was standing by the edge of the arena. Arden was in the whitest, tightest breeches Georgie had ever seen, and her hair was loose and flowing over her shoulders. She waved at James and he trotted his horse over to her, and then, in full view of everyone, he vaulted down off his horse and kissed her.

"Georgie?" Alice said. "Georgie, are you OK?"

"Not really," Georgie admitted.

"Honestly, you just need to forget him," Daisy said bluntly.

Georgie knew it was true. She just hoped that the day would come soon when James Kirkwood could no longer break her heart.

Chapter Ten

Georgie's alarm went off at five-thirty a.m. on Saturday. She could hear the groans from Alice in the bed opposite her as she struggled to get up.

"How does Tara expect us to train at six-thirty in the morning?" Alice whined as the two girls dragged themselves to the bathroom.

The bathrooms in Badminton House were massive – there were eight showers to accommodate the forty girls who lived there. But there was no queue for the showers at this hour.

On the outside, Badminton House was a gracious old building, two-storeys high, painted pale blue with scarlet trim around the door and window frames like the ribbons on a Southern Belle's gown. The showjumping squad members gathered on the front veranda and Georgie, Alice and Daisy waited while Kendal, Amy and Karen pulled on their boots – and then the six girls headed for the stables to saddle up for more training.

It was still dark and as they walked up the driveway, the girls pulled the sleeves of their school jerseys down over their fingers to keep warm, their breath making little puffs of steam in the chilly air.

Even on a Saturday at Blainford, students were meant to wear uniforms if they were on the school grounds. For training, the Badminton House girls wore their usual navy school jodhpurs, navy Blainford school jerseys and polo shirts in their house colours, the same brilliant scarlet as the trim on the windows of Badminton House.

Georgie was the only team member riding a school horse, and so, while the others headed into the stables to get their horses out of the loose boxes, Georgie grabbed her halter out of the tack room and walked to the paddock to catch Belle. The mare had been rolling as usual and even with her rug on she had managed to get herself completely covered in mud. Georgie only had enough time to give her a brisk brush to remove the worst of it and get Belle's saddle on as Tara was already waiting in the arena.

"Let's talk team tactics again," Tara said. "I'm glad I decided not to discuss anything in the arena in front of Heath and his boys on Monday, because I've just seen the draw for the knockout round. We're going to be competing against Burghley House."

There was a collective groan from the squad. Burghley were possibly the toughest opponents in the entire competition.

"This means our tactics have to change," Tara told the girls. "If we had drawn a team like Stars of Pau then I'd have said we could win by concentrating on getting good, solid clear rounds. But against Burghley, such a conservative approach won't work. They'll go clear and beat us on time faults, unless we can outwit them at their own game."

She eyed up the six riders in front of her. "Those of you who do not have your back protectors on, I need you to return to the stables and get changed. We're about to practise speed circuits and I want you all in full body armour."

While Amy and Kendal went to get their back protectors, the other riders warmed up, doing serpentines along the length of the arena while Tara set up the jumps. She was erecting a line of seven fences down the middle of the arena, just as she'd done at their Wednesday session. There was a double stride in between each jump.

As Kendal and Amy came back to join them, Tara called the girls to her. "I want you to ride the grid – but I only want you to go over every second jump. So jump a fence, then steer your horse around the next one, jump the one after that, and so on."

She looked at the riders. "One at time, please – Kendal, you first."

As Kendal dodged and weaved her way through the jumps, Tara yelled out instructions. "Swerve around the fence smoothly. Don't yank your horse around," she told Kendal. "Make the lines smooth and accurate. Aim for the centre of the jump. Now swerve again! Excellent!"

At first, the riders found it hard. Amy had trouble when Sandy refused at the second jump. "You didn't have enough impulsion! Make it clear when you are intending to jump," Tara told her. "Legs on! That's better."

Tara let the riders go through at their own speed twice each and then she put the pressure on.

"I'm timing you," she told them. "Keep jumping every second fence and maintain your rhythm, watch your canter leads, but go as fast as you can. This is against the clock."

In her first speed dash through the jumps, Daisy came to grief. Her Irish Hunter Village Voice was a long-backed horse, which meant he had a big jump in him, but was hard to steer around the turns at top speed. When Daisy turned in too tight on jump number three, Village Voice decided he didn't want to go and veered out dramatically to the side instead. Daisy went flying. Her body landed hard against the coloured rails, knocking the top two to the ground as she fell.

"I'm fine," she insisted, getting up quickly and

dusting herself off. Fortunately, the back protector had shielded her from the worst of the fall – without it she would probably have ended up with a couple of broken ribs. Instead, she was straight back on Village Voice and this time she was prepared in plenty of time before the jump, making sure that she didn't repeat her mistake.

Tara drilled her squad vigorously over the jumps, not cutting the girls any slack for their mistakes, making sure that they kept their horses on form the whole time. When Belle got a little lax with her hind legs and took a rail out three times in a row, Tara responded by raising all the fences by almost half a metre each.

"She's not respecting the jumps because they're too low for her to bother with," Tara reasoned. "Come through again, Georgie."

Once the fences were big enough, Belle flew them without putting a hoof out of place.

It was 8 a.m. – they had been training solidly for an hour and a half – when Tara finally looked down at her watch and declared that it was time to call it a day.

"Nice work, girls; go and give your horses a wash-down," Tara told them.

"A wash-down?" Alice flopped over William's neck and slid to the ground to lead him out of the arena. "I think I need a lie-down first! That just about killed me!"

"There's no time for lie-downs," Georgie groaned. "We need to hurry to the dining hall before breakfast finishes."

They were walking to the gates of the arena, when they saw a group of riders heading towards them.

"It looks like Adelaide House is also having an early training session," Daisy said.

"Is that Hans Schockelmann with them?" Georgie asked.

The legendary showjumping superstar, whose employment as team coach had caused so much controversy, was tall, leggy and lean as a cat. He was dressed in khaki breeches and brown leather boots and he had way too much gel in his strawberry blonde hair.

As he strode purposefully across the arena, Georgie

remembered what Alice had told her – the rumour about Hans dumping Tara Kelly before the School Formal all those years ago. She watched as Hans caught sight of their instructor. There was something about his forced grin and the theatrical way he threw his arms open in greeting that made it clear he was trying too hard.

"Tara! Tara Kelly!" Hans gushed. "How long has it been? Twenty years? They said you'd changed since then – and they were right. Just look at you!"

"Hello, Hans," Tara replied coolly. "We've just finished with the arena. It's all yours."

Hans wasn't going to be deterred. He lunged forward to clasp Tara in an embrace and give her a kiss on the cheek, but Tara swerved to the side. She ducked under his arms, and without giving him a second look, she strode out of the arena.

"So," Alice said as she watched their instructor storm off towards the stable block, "I'm guessing that the rumour about Hans and Tara is true."

Daisy nodded. "It looks like we have another reason for wanting to beat Adelaide House now."

Georgie stared over at Kennedy and Arden, who were mounted up beside Hans. "I already have two good reasons," she replied. "Come on, let's go get some breakfast. I'm starved."

On Sunday, Georgie rode Belle down the driveway and along the main avenue, lined on both sides with oak trees and black post-and-rail fences, until she reached the wrought-iron front gates of Blainford Academy. Here she turned to the left and headed down the road that led towards Pleasant Hill and Clemency Farm.

Riley was in the yard when she arrived. "So how have you and Belle been getting along this week?"

He stepped forward to stroke the mare on her dark muzzle.

"Pretty good," Georgie said. "We're doing really well in showjumping."

Riley led the way through the stables to the round pen. "We'll start in here again today. You can keep your reins this time," he smiled.

Georgie no longer felt resistant to Riley's methods and

she spent the next hour really listening and trying to do what Riley said, even though it often seemed to be the complete opposite to her own instinct. Whenever Belle surged forward and she wanted to snatch at the reins, Riley would tell her to stay still and quiet. If she took her legs off, Riley would tell her to put them on again. He didn't focus on the horse but spent all his time telling Georgie how to improve her position and relax in the saddle. "Some people like to fix horses," Riley explained. "I always say if you can fix the rider then the horse will be just fine."

Georgie was really pleased with her progress, and had been expecting a little more enthusiasm from Riley. But he seemed like he wasn't entirely happy.

"You're still thinking the wrong way," he told Georgie. "You think you need to hold this mare back, but what you really need to learn to do is let go."

"But Riley," Georgie argued, "it's OK to let go in a round pen, but on the cross-country course she'll just bolt!"

"Well, maybe you should let her!" Riley said, looking totally serious. "Georgie, when you've got a hot-headed horse like this one you can use up all their energy and your own by fighting them. By the time they get to the end of the cross-country they're exhausted and they've got no strength left for jumping the final fences. That's when you're putting yourself and your horse in danger. It's better to let go and stay with them."

"Yeah," Georgie sighed. "That's easy to say, but out there on the course when there's a fence right in front of you that's as big as a house, it's only natural to want to pull up…"

"I get that," Riley agreed. "It can be hard to let them gallop and…"

He looked at Georgie. "Hey, you know what? If you need galloping practice you should come and ride with me at Keeneland."

"You mean on the racetrack?"

"Sure," Riley said. "You could come and exercise the horses with me. It'll give you a chance to open up the throttle for once."

"You expect me to ride in one of those crazy, tiny little saddles with my knees tucked up to my armpits?"

"What's the matter?" Riley teased. "Are you scared?"

"No!" Georgie insisted.

"Great," Riley said. "Then I'll see you at the track."

Georgie had no idea how late it was getting until she noticed the sun sinking in the sky and the clouds on the horizon turning apricot and gold. As she turned down the road that led to the main gates of Blainford, she began to panic. On weekends all boarders had to be back at Blainford by five p.m. when the main gates were locked. What if she was too late already? She pressed Belle into a trot, her heart racing. She had no idea what she would do if they were locked out.

Georgie knew they were getting closer to the school boundary when the fencelines beside the road suddenly changed from white post-and-rail to black. Keeping the rails alongside her, she cantered on the grass verge beside the road until she reached a grove of trees known as the Drover's Dell. The paths through the dell were narrow, which meant that she had to trot from here, but it was a short cut of sorts. When she finally emerged back out the other side, she could now see the pale blue wrought-iron school gates ahead of her.

Georgie's heart soared when she saw there was a prefect at the gates. He must be locking up for the night!

"Wait!" Georgie yelled out. "Wait for me!"

She trotted along the tarmac towards the gates, waving. Georgie couldn't believe her luck – making it back just in time. She could see the boy had his head lowered, working the keys in the gate lock to let her in.

"Thanks," she called out. "I'm really sorry. I was running late…"

And then Georgie saw who it was.

Conrad Miller gave the lock a final twist and then removed his keys. He looked down at his watch.

"Five minutes past five," he said icily. "Gates are closed at five p.m."

Georgie pleaded, but Conrad was deaf to her cries as he turned his horse and rode back up the avenue towards the school, leaving Georgie sitting there, stunned, exhausted and locked out of Blainford for the night.

Chapter Eleven

*S*tuck outside the gates, Georgie rode up and down the fenceline and considered her options. She could try riding back to Clemency Farm, but it was getting dark and she didn't have any reflective gear or a torch so it wouldn't be safe on the roads. She didn't have a phone or any way of contacting anyone. There was nothing to do but stay here and wait.

Two hours later she was beginning to give up hope when a car finally pulled up at the gates. Georgie and Belle were caught in the headlights and a few moments later the door of the Chevrolet swung open, and then she heard a familiar voice in the darkness. "Georgie? Is that you?"

"Kenny!" Georgie was so relieved to see him.

"What are you doing out here at this time of night?"

"I got locked out."

"Well, what did you go and do that for?" Kenny shook his head as he stepped up to the wrought-iron gates, producing a ring of keys from his pocket.

"You better lead your horse and follow me," Kenny told her once they were inside. "It's too dark to ride."

Kenny drove at a crawl, his headlights illuminating the path as Georgie led Belle alongside her. It took ages to get back to the stables, but Georgie was just grateful to be through the gates and back on Blainford grounds. She knew she'd be in trouble. It was against the rules for a student to be out past the five o'clock curfew. Conrad had no doubt already put her name down for fatigues and she would be forced to do some humiliating task like cleaning the school toilets. At least Kenny didn't seem interested in taking her to task. He even offered to look after Belle when they arrived at the stables. "I'll feed her and turn her out. You get back to your boarding house and let them know you're OK. They'll be getting worried about you," he insisted.

If Georgie was hoping to slip back into Badminton

House unnoticed, she was out of luck. Mrs Birdwell, her house mistress, was waiting on the doorstep with Mrs Dubois.

"I'm sorry, I'm a bit late," was all Georgie could offer.

"Miss Parker," Mrs Dubois said. "Two hours is more than 'a bit'. Weekend leave at Blainford is a privilege, not a right…"

"But Conrad Miller locked me out on purpose. I was only five minutes late to the gates!"

Mrs Dubois held up her hand. "I don't want to hear your excuses. Rules are rules. I'm letting you off with a warning, Miss Parker, but next time you will have all your leave cancelled and a letter will be sent home to your father. Am I making myself clear?"

"Yes, Mrs Dubois."

Once she was inside, the Badminton House girls swarmed around to find out what had happened.

"Typical Conrad!" Alice fumed. "I bet he loved locking the gates on you." She turned to her sister. "I can't believe you used to go out with him."

"It was, like, two dates!" Kendal objected. "It's not like

he was my boyfriend." She hated to be reminded of the fact that she had briefly been keen on Conrad, so Alice got great pleasure out of bringing it up.

"Don't get mad with him," was Daisy's advice. "Get even."

On Saturday they were up against Burghley in the knockout round. If Georgie wanted to even the score with Conrad then she would get her chance – in the showjumping arena.

The week that followed was plagued by patchy autumn weather. At cross-country on Monday afternoon the rain was so torrential that the class was a disaster. Tara had planned to work on arrowhead combinations, but after Belle and Georgie did an awful mud slide, mistiming the jump and crashing right into a narrow fence, Tara decided to call it quits.

"I'm not risking riders and horses right before the House Showjumping," she told the class.

For the rest of the week most classes were held in the

indoor arena to try and preserve the outdoor arenas from getting too churned up. Even so, by Friday morning the sand surfaces were still soggy underfoot.

"You'll need to put large studs in your horses' shoes to help with their grip," Tara told her team as they tacked up that morning. "I don't want any of you sliding over – that could lose us the competition."

Tara didn't even try to disguise her comment as concern for their safety – all she was worried about was winning.

"Gather round, girls," Tara told them. "I want to have a quick talk about tactics."

The girls formed a circle around Tara, sitting down on the stack of hay bales at the end of the stables.

"Do you all understand how the scoring system works today?" Tara asked. "You'll be racing the clock and trying for a clear round. There are six of you, but only the five best scores will be added up to give us our team tally. That means one of the scores – the worst one, obviously – gets discarded from the final total."

The girls nodded that they understood.

"As I've said before," Tara continued, "Burghley will

aim for clear rounds, so if the score is tied, this competition will be won or lost on time faults. It's imperative that we come out and dominate the competition right from the start."

Tara looked at the girls. "Kendal, I'm putting you up first. You have the most experience, so I want you to go in there as our trailblazer. It's your job to figure out where the problems on this course lie and pass on that knowledge to the team. I expect all of you to listen to her advice once she comes out of the arena."

The girls nodded.

"Alice, you'll follow Kendal. Will is a very safe jumper. I need you to get points on the board. Your aim will be to go clear – don't push your luck for the sake of speed. Daisy, you will follow her and do the same – Village Voice is not built for speedy turns so don't take too many risks. The main thing I'm looking for is safe clear rounds."

Tara turned to Amy and Karen. "If the other girls put in solid clear rounds ahead of you, then it is time for you to deliver the speed. I want both of you to go around that course as fast as you can."

Georgie raised her hand nervously. "Ummm, Tara? What about me?"

Tara turned to her. "You're the last to go, Georgie. When the time comes, I'll tell you what to do."

As the girls finished saddling up, Georgie felt a tight knot growing in her belly. So much was riding on this sudden-death knockout – and she would be riding last! She could feel the weight of expectation from Tara, her House and her team mates.

Alone in the loose box with Belle, she did a final check on her gear, making sure her girth was tight enough, checking the noseband on her bridle.

She spoke softly to the mare as she worked, Belle's ears swivelling back and forth, as if she was listening to every word. Georgie had already spent hours grooming her that morning. She had plaited the mare's jet-black mane in tight rosettes and bound them with white tape to match the white bandages on Belle's legs. The contrast against the bay mare's black points was dramatic.

"She looks gorgeous," Alice said as she met up with Georgie in the stables.

"William does too," Georgie said. Alice hadn't plaited

Will's mane, but it was freshly pulled so that it was short and erect like the plume on a Roman centurion's helmet and she had gamgee bandaged his legs too.

Daisy walked up to join the two girls. "Tara is waiting for us beside the arena," she told them. "She's ready to walk the course."

Georgie nodded nervously and Alice took a deep breath. "Let's do it," she said.

There were three outdoor arenas and each of them had a jumping course erected with flags in the house colours of the competing teams at the gates. Adelaide House's pink flags flew beside the purple of Stars of Pau at arena number one. Lexington versus Luhmuhlen had their yellow and black flags flying at number two. And Burghley and Badminton would be competing in arena three – the scarlet of Badminton House standing out against the ice blue of Burghley's banner.

"Riders," Mrs Dickins-Thomson addressed the assembled teams. "You have twenty minutes to walk the course."

The girls strode into the arena with Tara leading the way on foot, walking through the exact route she expected them to follow, stepping out the correct number of strides to take between fences.

There were twelve jumps in the course, all between a metre-twenty and a metre-thirty in height. They were substantial fences – "big enough to cause trouble" as Tara put it. As they walked around together, short cuts and tactics were talked about in whispery voices. They had to be careful what they said as the Burghley boys, led by Heath Brompton, were also walking the course at the same time.

Georgie tried to keep her eyes on the jumps, to focus her attention on what Tara was telling her, but it wasn't easy. As she walked around the jumps she was aware of James Kirkwood's eyes following her. He was flanked on either side by Conrad Miller and Andrew Hurley. Their stares gave Georgie the creeps, which was probably the intention. When she saw Damien Danforth, she gave him a smile and he muttered hello to her. It was enough to rile Conrad, who began making squawking noises at Damien. "Seagull!" she heard Conrad sneer at Damien. "Caw!

Caw!" She saw Damien's expression darken while Andrew and Conrad fell about laughing.

Suddenly Georgie heard someone calling out her name. "Hey, Parker."

She turned around and saw James Kirkwood. He'd broken away from his group of boys and was walking towards her. He was wearing his white showjumping breeches and ice-blue polo shirt, and the colours made his tanned skin and blond hair look amazing. He stood right in front of her and Georgie felt her heart beating like crazy. What did James want? Why was he talking to her all of a sudden?

"Hey, uhhh, I, ummm, wanted to ask you a question," James said.

Georgie tried to act cool, but her voice wavered as she replied, "W-what sort of question?"

"I wanted to know if anyone had asked you to the School Formal," James said. Georgie was transfixed by his eyes. James Kirkwood was so handsome. She'd nearly forgotten just how gorgeous he was.

"No…" she managed to get the word out, "no one's asked me yet."

She looked at him and held her breath. "Why?"

James smiled, but there was something different about the grin this time. Something she hadn't seen before.

"Oh, no reason," he said. "Conrad was wondering if you'd managed to scrape up a date." And with that he turned his back. "Enjoy the competition!"

There were snorts of laughter and Georgie looked over to see Conrad and Andrew Hurley falling about the place as if they'd just witnessed something hilarious. Conrad muttered something to James and then gave him a high five as he looked at Georgie. They'd sent James over just to rattle her!

"Ignore them." Georgie heard Daisy hiss in her ear, then felt her team mate's hand wrapped around her arm, pulling her away. "Don't let them put you off. They're only messing with you because they know that we can beat them."

Georgie was shaking by the time she reached the sidelines and mounted up on Belle.

"Are you OK?" Alice asked her. "Is Conrad being a jerk again?"

"I'm fine," Georgie said. "I just wish they'd leave me alone."

They were interrupted by the sound of a bell ringing

and Tara Kelly calling out, "Kendal! You're up first! Into the arena now!"

Over the next half-hour, Tara's theory worked perfectly. The Burghley riders had been planning to dominate the competition by being the fastest around the course, but when Kendal Dupree slam-dunked a clear round in a very tight time of one minute and forty-three seconds, the boys suddenly realised they had a different type of contest on their hands.

Damien Danforth was the first rider up for Burghley and Georgie had been pleased for his sake when he went clear as well, only slightly behind Kendal's time at one minute and forty-seven seconds.

Riding in positions two and three, Alice and Daisy stuck to the game plan. They both rode safe, clear rounds and put points on the board, but their times were much slower than Kendal's. Still, they were more than holding their own against Burghley. Andrew Hurley had a very fast time, going like a bat out of hell around the jumps, but he dropped a rail for four faults. Nicholas Laurent did the same, going far too fast and dropping more rails for another eight faults.

Badminton House had the advantage as Amy entered the arena. She tipped her hat to the judges and waited for the bell, then pushed her horse through the flags at a brisk canter. But right from the very start you could see that she wasn't on form. Sandhurst Debonair virtually ran through the first fence, mistiming it and taking the jump on a bad stride, knocking down three rails.

"That's still only four faults," Alice pointed out. "Burghley have twelve so far."

Unfortunately, Burghley's twelve were about to be surpassed. Amy took out the top rails on another three fences for an abysmal score of sixteen.

"I'm so sorry." She was almost in tears as she met her team mates on the sidelines. "I don't know what went wrong!"

"You had a bad day," Tara said. "It happens to all of us. Don't dwell on it. We're still in with a good chance."

Georgie knew what Tara was thinking. She still had two riders to come. With any luck both Karen and Georgie would go clear, and then they could discard Amy's score.

The girls watched with knots in their bellies as the fourth Burghley rider also put in a poor round for a massive twelve faults. His score would be discarded for sure.

"Good luck, Karen!" The Badminton House team were yelling their support as Karen Lockhart rode into the arena on Rolling Rock. But it was not to be Karen's day either. Rolling Rock took a strange dislike to fence number three, the bright orange-coloured rails with a white picket fence used at the base as fill. The mare refused point-blank to jump the first time, and when she refused a second time despite Karen's desperate urgings, the bell was rung. Elimination!

On the sidelines, the Badminton House girls all worked it out. Karen's elimination meant that she would be the discard score and so Amy's sixteen faults would be included in their final tally. They were sitting on a score of at least sixteen, no matter what. The girls had their hearts in their mouths as Conrad Miller rode into the arena.

"Where's a voodoo doll when you need one?" Alice groaned as she watched Conrad going clear over fence after fence. Georgie didn't want to be a bad sport, but as she watched Conrad all she could think was that she wished a rail would fall. Just one lousy rail.

As Conrad came into the final treble at the end of the course, he looked untouchable. But then the unthinkable happened. His horse dropped his front legs just a little and the sound of poles rocking in the sockets was followed by the crash of rails falling. The jump was down! Conrad Miller had four faults. With just one rider from each house to come, both teams now sat on sixteen faults each.

By the time Georgie entered the ring the Badminton House girls were going wild, waving flags and calling out her name, shouting advice. But as she entered the arena Georgie completely blocked them out. It was as if the whole world fell away and all that remained was the showjumping course in front of her.

The only thing on her mind was a clear round – and the last words Tara had said: "No time to play it safe. I want you to go as fast as you can. Now get in there and finish it!"

Georgie came through the flags with Belle in full stride and they barrelled at the first fence. The mare leapt like a gazelle and Georgie was already looking to the next fence in mid-air.

It was a text-book round and by the time Belle and Georgie were halfway around the course they were totally in the zone and working so perfectly as a team, it was like poetry. There was only one hairy moment when Georgie cut the corner into the oxer and took it far too tightly. She had to rely entirely on Belle's natural athleticism and luckily the mare somehow gathered herself up in a very short stride and made a fantastic jump. With disaster averted they headed for home, taking the upright rails and facing down for the treble. Over fence one, hup, then two, then, hup-hup two big strides and over fence three – they were clear and galloping through the flags. Their time, a stunning one minute forty-two!

But it wasn't over yet. The last rider was still to come. If James Kirkwood could go clear and beat Georgie's time, then it would be the end of the tournament for Badminton House.

There was a silence from the sidelines as James rode into the arena. You could almost hear the crowd holding their breath with every fence that James took. For once, the cheeky lopsided grin was nowhere to be seen and he wore a grim mask of concentration as he took the first two fences, then the third and the fourth. He was still clear and his dark brown gelding was going at breakneck speed.

In the same corner where Georgie had cut it too fine, James came in towards the oxer on a tight angle and at the last minute you could see him panic and try to check his stride. Beneath him, his horse grunted with the effort as he took off far too close to clear the rail. And in a clattering of wood and metal falling to the ground it was done. The jump was down! Burghley were defeated and Badminton House were through to the next round!

Chapter Twelve

*T*he guard at the entrance gates shone his torch on the old Chevrolet as it pulled up. He peered in and smiled at the man behind the wheel. "G'morning, Kenny," he said. "You can go right on through."

"Thanks, Earl," Kenny gave the guard a wave as he rolled on through the gates towards the ivy-covered limestone buildings up ahead. In the passenger seat beside him, Georgie peered out into the darkness. She could make out the shadowy shapes of horses and hear the clean chime of their metal shoes against the concrete surface of the stable block, and the sound of men's voices carrying in the cold early morning air.

This was Keeneland Park Race Course. "One of the

most famous tracks in the whole of bluegrass county," Kenny told Georgie as he drove on. "Secretariat was ridden at Keeneland," he added, looking at Georgie as if this should mean something. Then he sighed when he saw her blank expression.

"You telling me you ain't heard of Secretariat?" asked Kenny in amazement.

Georgie shook her head.

"What about Citation?" Kenny offered. "He won the triple crown. You musta heard of Citation? Or how about Seattle Slew?"

Georgie shook her head again. "I'm not much into racing Kenny; sorry."

But even as she said this, she knew that it wasn't entirely true. Sure, she didn't know the names of all the famous racehorses of Lexington, but she could still appreciate the beauty of a horse in full gallop, bearing down on the finish line, trying his heart out while his jockey dressed in coloured silks urged him on.

There were no coloured silks this morning at Keeneland. The jockeys wore old jerseys and sweatshirts with their boots and breeches. They sat on their horses, telling jokes and smoking cigarettes as they waited for their turn on the track.

Leaning against the railings were the trainers. They wore heavy coats and had binoculars hanging around their necks and stopwatches clasped in their hands. As the jockeys walked their horses around in the morning mist, the trainers called out instructions to them.

"Breeze him over eight furlongs," Georgie heard a man in a grey overcoat instructing his jockey as he wrestled with a big chestnut wearing blinkers and a hood. "We'll see how he feels after that."

Beside the railings, another jockey sat on a streamlined dark bay, also wearing blinkers and a hood. He looked over at Kenny and Georgie and gave them a wave, then rode over to join them.

"Hey, Georgie!" It was Riley.

"Are you all set to ride?" he asked her.

"Umm, I thought maybe I could just watch today," Georgie said. "Maybe I can ride next time?"

Now that she was at the racetrack surrounded by real jockeys and trainers she felt self-consciously out of her depth.

Riley shook his head. "No way," he said firmly. "Come on, follow me."

At the stables a solidly built man wearing a brown wool jersey and baggy corduroy breeches came over towards them leading a pretty young chestnut filly. The man looked so much like Kenny, Georgie guessed straight away that this must be Riley's father.

"John Conway." The man reached out and grasped Georgie's hand and smiled. "You must be Georgie. Riley told me you were coming. I've got Clarise here ready for you."

Georgie looked at the chestnut filly. She was so finely built she didn't look like a horse so much as a gazelle, all bone and sinew, with the delicate, wide-eyed face of a woodland faun.

"Clarise is up for a race in a few weeks' time," Riley's dad told Georgie. "You can breeze her over eight furlongs and then give her a cool-down, OK?"

"Dad," Riley laughed, "you're gonna have to hire a translator. Georgie's never ridden trackwork before."

"Oh," John Conway's face broke into a broad grin. "Sorry about that. When I say I want you to breeze her, I mean take her at a gallop, but hold her back at about half speed." He pointed over to the racetrack. "You see those posts at the side of the track? Each one marks a furlong. A furlong is about an eighth of a mile – so eight furlongs is a whole mile – that'll take you right the way round the track. Trot Clarise to the first marker then let her gallop, just breeze her like I said, and then bring her back to a trot and cool her off."

He legged her up and Georgie took the reins and tucked her feet into the stirrups of the racing saddle. It felt so weird having her knees scrunched high above the horse's withers!

"You'll get used to it," Riley said as he walked alongside her on the dark bay, whose name turned out to be Lafayette. They rode past maple trees with their leaves aflame, and by the time Georgie reached the track she'd begun to adjust to her new position.

"Stick to the rail," Riley advised. "I'll ride outside you on Lafayette. Look out for other jockeys – just go wide if you want to overtake anyone."

Georgie gave a hollow laugh. "I don't think I'm ready to do any overtaking!"

179

It felt strange doing a rising trot sitting so high up, and Georgie actually found it easier when she asked Clarise to move up into a gallop. Even though Clarise was light-framed, her gallop was powerful and strong and she pulled Georgie forward as she snatched at the reins. Georgie found herself really having to hold on to keep the filly at half-speed as instructed.

On the outside of her, Riley was staying close and she could see he was holding Lafayette back too. He gave her a nod and a grin to let her know she was doing OK.

As they came past the stands she could hear the steady cadence of the filly's hoofbeats echoing through the empty grandstand, and she wondered what it would be like to be here when the stands were full and there were other horses racing against you. Right now, with just Riley beside her, it still felt amazing. She could hear Clarise's hooves pounding a four-beat against the soft loam of the track, could feel the filly's muscles moving beneath her in beautiful symmetry as they galloped on. Ahead of her, there were enough grandstand lights on to illuminate the track through the darkness of the early morning. She did as Riley said and kept the mare hugging the white rail, keeping her at half-speed.

Even at a slow gallop, Georgie could feel the pent-up power in the mare. She could sense the speed that Clarise was capable of. As the furlong posts whizzed past, Georgie felt the mare leaning on the reins, wanting to be let go.

"Steady there, Clarise," she murmured as she kept a firm grip on the leggy chestnut. They had come all the way around the track and so at the eighth furlong marker, Georgie did what John Conway had told her to do, pulling the Thoroughbred back to a trot once more. Clarise objected, bearing down on the bit and trying to pull the reins slack, but Georgie was firm with her and eventually she came back down to a trot. Riley was alongside her all the way.

"You handled her just fine," he said approvingly. "Well done."

Georgie was flushed pink and she had a huge grin on her face. "That was much more fun than I expected!"

"I told you so," Riley said. He looked over at his father,

who stood waiting for them beside the railing. "Dad! I think Georgie should be the one to take Tally out today."

John Conway frowned. "Talisman's got a race tomorrow at Churchill Downs, Riley – this is his last training session."

"I know," Riley said. He gave Georgie a grin. "Georgie's a Blainford girl. She can handle it."

John Conway considered it for a moment. "OK," he said. "Talisman is your ride. If you want to put Georgie up on him instead then that's your call."

"Come on," Riley said to Georgie. "This should be fun."

Georgie wasn't so sure that this was her idea of fun at all. As John Conway legged her up on to the back of the enormous seventeen-hand black colt she could see the whites of Talisman's eyes. He already had a gleam of sweat on his sleek black coat. This was the horse she had seen Riley riding the day that they met. He was highly strung, in peak racing condition, and as hot as a rocket.

"This is his final workout before the stakes race," John

Conway told her, "I want you to take him out on the track and blow him out."

"Blowing him out means taking him as fast as he can go," Riley explained as he led Georgie back towards the track. "We're talking race speed, Georgie. No matter what happens, don't hold him back. Push him up into a hard-out gallop right at the start and then when you reach the sixth furlong post, ask him for a little bit more, OK?"

"Uhhh," Georgie was nervous. "What if I mess up?"

"You won't," Riley said. "No trotting at the start either – let Tally loose straight into a gallop, then push him at the sixth furlong and hang on."

As Talisman skipped and danced out on to the track, Georgie could feel her heart hammering in her chest like crazy. She took a deep breath and tried to stop her hands from shaking, wiping her palms so she could take a better grip on the reins. At that moment she wanted to turn Talisman around and take him back to Riley and tell him that she couldn't do this. It was too scary being on a real-live racehorse that was about to hit top speed. But the other jockeys and their trainers were milling about, watching her, waiting for her to take the big, black horse out on to the track. Somehow she knew that there was no backing out of this. Like Riley had said, she was a Blainford girl, after all.

After warming Talisman up with a couple of little trots back and forth, Georgie turned the big black horse to face the first furlong post. She looked over to the railing where Riley was standing with his dad and waited until he gave her the nod.

"Come on, Tally," Georgie said, bracing herself in her stirrups. "Let's see what you can do."

As Talisman broke from a standstill into a gallop Georgie was ready for him. She felt the black colt surge forward beneath her and instead of holding him back, she swallowed her fear and let go.

She was off and racing! Talisman's hooves were pounding out their frantic rhythm beneath her on the soft sandy soil, getting faster and faster with every stride. Every fibre of Georgie's being was telling her to slow down. This horse was too fast! If she fell off at this speed it would be disastrous. As they reached the second furlong post she wanted more than anything to pull back on the reins. But she resisted the urge and kept calm, staying with the movement of the black horse beneath her.

They were hard against the rail as they came into the turn at the fourth furlong, Talisman was galloping flat-out, when Georgie saw a grey colt running on the track ahead of them. They were gaining on the other horse fast and in just a few strides they would be alongside it!

Remembering what Riley had told her, Georgie pulled Talisman wide away from the rails. The big black horse's stride never faltered as they swept around, drawing up alongside the grey Thoroughbred.

The jockey on the grey horse seemed surprised to see Talisman pull up alongside him. They were neck and neck, and having the grey horse to race against seemed to ignite something in Talisman. He stepped his strides up and lengthened out so that in just three lengths they were edging ahead of the grey and against the rails once more.

Georgie stayed with her horse, rocking low over his withers. Her eyes were streaming tears from the wind in her face and her heart was pounding so hard she could hardly breathe, but she hung on as they bore down on the sixth furlong marker.

As soon as she was alongside the marker, Georgie did exactly as Riley had told her. She loosened the reins off and pressed her hands against the colt's black neck, then she tapped him with her heels, calling his name, asking for even more speed. Talisman responded brilliantly, and the ground was swallowed up by the horse's massive strides. Georgie's vision turned blurry and blood was pounding in her ears. She'd never been this fast on a horse before in her life, but instead of feeling scared, she felt free. As they thundered down the home straight, Georgie leaned down low over the horse's neck and yelled words of encouragement, urging him on. Her voice was lost on the wind, but Talisman gave a final surge, his strides stretching out to the very limits as they hit the eighth furlong.

John Conway watched the big black horse pass the final marker and at the precise moment he saw the colt's nose cross the line he flicked down the button on his stopwatch. He looked at the time and shook his head in amazement. Riley's little friend had just ridden Talisman over eight furlongs in one minute thirty-four. It was the fastest time the black colt had ever recorded at Keeneland. It might even be fast enough to win the meet at Churchill Downs! The girl trotted Talisman back again to greet him with a wide smile on her pretty face.

"That was so cool!" Georgie beamed. "I loved it. Thank you for letting me ride him."

"Any time," John Conway said. He cast another surreptitious glance at his stopwatch, just to make sure he'd clocked that time right.

"Any time at all."

That morning at the Keeneland Park track was one of the best of Georgie's life. After she'd finished riding Talisman, she watched as Riley breezed another two young horses – the grey and the bay that she'd seen in the boxes at Clemency Farm on her first visit. Then she'd joined him and the other jockeys in a big, bustling kitchen beside the stables for breakfast.

Georgie had piled her plate high with bacon, maple syrup and waffles, and tucked in happily. As she ate, she noticed that many of the hardened track riders around her weren't even touching the huge buffet table groaning with food, making do with black coffee and nothing else.

"They're on diets," Riley explained in a whisper. "They need to stay thin enough to make racing weight."

While Georgie worked her way through two helpings of the waffles, she listened to the jockeys telling tall tales around the table, trying to outdo each other with epic accounts of great races won or lost.

Even though most of them were much older, Riley seemed to fit right in. He joined in the talk, whilst being respectful of the senior jockeys.

"Hey, Riley," one of the others at the table called over, "Ain't you gonna introduce us to your girlfriend?"

Riley's smile suddenly disappeared. "She's not my girlfriend. Georgie's just doing a bit of trackwork for me."

The other jockeys went on talking after that, but Riley looked uncomfortable. He picked up his plate and took it to the sink.

"We should go now," he said to Georgie.

As they walked back towards the Chevrolet, Riley stuck his hands in his pockets. "Sorry about what they said back there," he said. "I didn't tell them you were my girlfriend or anything. Those guys just make stuff up."

Georgie smiled. "They do seem to like telling stories."

"Oh, yeah," Riley rolled his eyes, "I've heard all of those stories at least ten times. Mind you, they change every time they tell them."

Kenny was already in the front seat waiting for her. Georgie swung open the passenger door, then turned back to Riley to say her goodbyes.

"You did really good out on the track today," Riley smiled at her. "You really let go." He paused and then he said, "I think we're done, Georgie. After the way you handled Tally on that track, I don't think you need my help any more."

The smile disappeared from Georgie's face. "Oh," she said, trying to keep the hurt out of her voice. "Well, umm, OK then. Thanks."

"Maybe I'll see you around sometime?" Riley replied.

Riding trackwork this morning had been one of the

best times Georgie had ever had. She thought he'd had fun too. So why didn't Riley want to see her again?

Georgie suddenly realised that it wasn't just about the horses. She enjoyed being with him, hanging out. The thought of this being over, of it being the end made her stomach go funny inside.

"Yeah," Georgie said as she got into the Chevrolet. "See you around."

She slid over on the bench seat and Riley slammed the passenger door shut, gave her a wave through the window and turned to walk away back to the stables. Georgie sat for a moment, her heart racing, watching him go. Kenny had just put the car into gear and was about to set off when something inside of her snapped.

"Wait!" She opened the car door and called out after him, "Riley! Wait!"

Georgie leapt out of the car and ran across the grass. She was trembling with excitement and nerves as she stood there facing him. She was standing so close she could see a tiny cluster of perfect brown freckles across the bridge of Riley's crooked nose. Georgie gazed into his green eyes and almost lost her nerve.

"Yeah?" Riley smiled. "What is it?"

"I was just wondering," Georgie hesitated. She took a deep breath and then the words came tumbling out.

"Riley Conway, would you go to the School Formal with me?"

Chapter Thirteen

Georgie stared expectantly at Riley, waiting for his reply.

"What's a formal?" he said.

"Oh!" Georgie was flustered. "I should have explained that first! It's like a dance. There's one at school at the end of term and I was wondering if you would, you know, go with me?"

"A dance?" Riley frowned, "At Blainford?"

"Uh-huh," Georgie smiled.

"Does that mean getting dressed up in a suit?"

"Well," Georgie said, "I was planning on wearing a dress, but yes, you'd have to wear a suit."

Riley looked uncertain. He gazed down at his feet, avoiding Georgie's eyes. "I dunno… I'm not much of a dancer. It doesn't sound like my sort of thing, Georgie. I'm sorry."

Georgie's smile disappeared. "Oh, hey, no," she said, "I mean, sure, that's fine. I didn't really think you'd want to go, but that's OK. Really. OK. I better go now."

"Georgie, wait…" Riley began, but it was too late. Georgie ran back and jumped into the front seat of the Chevrolet, pulling the door shut after her, mortified with embarrassment.

"He turned you down?" Alice pulled a face. "What is going on? Are we so totally un-dateable that even Kenny's nephew won't go to the Formal with us?"

"He said it 'wasn't his sort of thing'," Georgie said as she threw herself down on the sofa in the Badminton House common room.

"The School Formal is only three weeks away and none of us have dates yet," Emily sighed.

"Actually," Daisy King said, putting down the eventing magazine she had been reading, "I've got a date."

"You've got a what?" Alice was stunned. "But you said

that the whole School Formal thing was pointless! You didn't even want to go!"

Daisy shrugged. "I know. But then I figured that since everyone else was going I might as well. And besides, I look really good in a prom dress."

"So who is it?" Emily wanted to know.

"Who is what?" Daisy replied.

"Don't mess with us, Daisy," Alice snapped. "You know what she means. Who's asked you to the Formal?"

"Oh," Daisy said airily. "I thought I'd said already." She looked at their expectant faces. "Nicholas Laurent."

"Wow," Emily Tait was thoroughly impressed. "He's so... so French!"

Alice groaned, "Well, duh, Emily – I think we've all noticed that!"

"The French are so sophisticated," Emily said, throwing herself on the sofa next to Daisy, who was trying to read her magazine again. "They speak the language of love!"

"I thought they spoke French," Georgie said.

Daisy sighed. "I'm not marrying him, Emily, he's just taking me to the Formal."

"I wish Alex would ask me," Emily looked wistful.

"Why don't you ask him?" Alice countered.

"Ohmygod, I couldn't!" Emily buried her head in a sofa cushion. "What if he said no?"

"Good point," Georgie groaned. "I wish I'd thought of that before I asked Riley."

"Even if we don't have dates," Alice continued, "we should get our dresses organised."

"What's the point in having something to wear to the Formal if no one has actually asked you to go?" Georgie said.

"Think about it this way," Alice said. "What if someone does ask you at the last minute and you don't have anything to wear?"

"OK," Emily said. "So where are we going to buy them from?"

"Selma's Second-timers," Alice said. "It's a vintage store in Lexington. Kendal bought her last two formal dresses from Selma's. She got a red silk chiffon one and it only cost her eight dollars. All she did was rip the lace off the bottom and it was perfect."

That night, Georgie emailed home to Lily, her best friend back in Little Brampton. She realised she hadn't emailed since the mid-term break so she had a lot to tell – all about James and the Kirkwood mansion, through to riding trackwork and asking Riley out. She'd barely clicked send when Lily's reply pinged back to her.

I don't hear from you for three whole weeks, Lily wrote, *and then I get an email saying you've split up with James! Last time you wrote you weren't even going out with him, so that qualifies as the world's shortest relationship!*

Lily was being her usual sympathetic self.

At least your boy troubles involve private jets and racehorses, Lily continued. *The closest I've got to boy trouble is Nigel Potts. I bought fish and chips from the Fish Pott last Friday night and Nigel was working on the till and when I got home there was an extra crabstick in my order! I think he fancies me, but he smells like a deep fryer. He's still in my class at school, but he keeps telling everyone that he is leaving as soon as he sits his GCSEs to "take on a role*

at the family firm" – which makes it sound like his dad is
Richard Branson when in fact he runs a chip shop! Well, he
needs to realise my love can't be bought with a crabstick…

Lily was right. Her love life was worse than
Georgie's.

By Monday morning it was clear that Formal Fever had
crept up on the whole of Blainford. Everywhere Georgie
looked there were clusters of girls gossiping about who
had asked them to the dance, and boys looking as if they
were about to throw up with the anxiety of doing the
asking.

"Tyler McGuane's asked Bunny Redpath, and Jenner
Philips is going with Blair Danner – but just as friends,
they're not dating or anything," Alice reported excitedly
as they took their seats in Ms Schmidt's class. "And…"
she whispered conspiratorially, glancing over at the
dressage geeks in the front row, "I heard that Karl
Mortensen asked Isabel Weiss!"

Isabel certainly seemed to have that golden glow that

a girl gets when she has a date for the Formal. Or at least Georgie imagined that was what she'd look like if she had a date – she wouldn't know since she still didn't have one herself.

As for Alice, everyone knew that she had been waiting patiently, ever since the dance was first mentioned, for Cameron to ask her. Everyone, it seemed, except Cameron.

Cameron and Alex Chang had both made it through the knockout stage with the Luhmuhlen House showjumping team and had been training after school on Tuesdays and Thursdays.

"Meanwhile, we're training on Mondays and Wednesdays and Saturdays," Alice complained to Georgie, "So I hardly ever see Cam. No wonder he hasn't asked me to the Formal. He hasn't had a chance."

"Maybe he doesn't realise that you want to go with him?" Georgie said. "Maybe you should drop a few hints?"

And so, as the girls walked to the dining room for lunch, Alice manoeuvred her way to Cameron's side. "Hey, Cam!" she said brightly.

"Hi, Alice," Cameron grinned. "How's your showjumping

training going? It's pretty cool that both our houses made the finals, huh?"

"Yeah," Alice agreed, "really cool…"

She could see Georgie and Emily watching her from across the quad, egging her on.

"So the School Formal is coming up—" Alice began.

"I know!" Cam said. "Hey, I wanted to ask you… what do you think about me wearing a tuxedo? Is it retro cool or should I just wear a suit?"

Alice was confused. "Ummm, a suit, I guess…"

"Or I could wear a kilt?" Cam suggested. "I've got one. It's in my clan tartan – black and red and green."

"I don't know, Cam," Alice said. "It might be OK in Scotland, but most girls here would probably prefer it if they were the only one in the couple wearing a skirt, you know?"

"Got you!" Cam said. "Good advice. No skirt. And what about corsages? Should they be like these big floral things or just a little wrist strap?"

"Orchids are always nice," Alice offered. "They're a reasonable size."

"Right," Cam said. "That's brilliant. Thanks, Alice."

"Listen, Cam—" Alice began, but he cut her off again.

"I'll catch up with you later, OK?" Cam said distractedly, looking across the quad. "I need to go talk to Kennedy before someone else gets in first." And Cameron was off and running.

Cameron was panting as he caught up with the showjumperettes in the lunch queue at the dining-hall door. Kennedy Kirkwood was holding court with Arden and Tori on either side, flanking her like obedient, well-groomed Afghan hounds.

"Hey, Kennedy," Cam smiled at her. "Can I ask you something?"

Kennedy shrugged. "I guess so. What is it?"

Cam cleared his throat. "I just wanted to ask you… ummm, whether you had a date for the Formal yet?"

Kennedy's eyes opened wide. "You're asking me to the Formal?"

"Well, yeah," Cameron said. Kennedy hesitated. "I won't wear a skirt," Cameron added hastily, "and I'll get you a reasonable-sized orchid."

"Wow," Kennedy said dryly. "When you put it that

way, you make it sound so tempting. Sorry, Kevin…"

"It's Cameron. My name is Cameron."

"O-K, whatever," Kennedy said, "I'm sorry *Cameron*, but as I was saying, I already have a date for the Formal."

"She already has a date!"

Cameron plonked his lunch tray down on the table next to Alice and flung himself down in his chair. He began to stab at his pasta in a menacing fashion. "How come I didn't know that? Who is he?"

"Does it matter?" Georgie said. "Just forget about it Cam, let it go." She was trying desperately to shut Cameron up. His talk wasn't exactly improving Alice's terrible mood. She was still in shock at what she described as 'the ultimate betrayal'.

"I mean, does Kennedy even really have a date or is that just her way of giving me the brush-off?" Cameron ranted. "She didn't even know my name! She called me Kevin!"

"Stop obsessing, Cam," Emily Tait said. "There are lots of other girls you could ask…"

"Hah!" Cameron gave a hollow laugh. "No way. I'm not setting myself up to be the guy that gets turned down twice. Way too embarrassing, thank you very much!"

He turned to Alice, "So I guess it's you and me then!"

Alice, who had been studiously concentrating on her pasta and trying desperately to ignore Cameron's ranting, suddenly looked up. "You and me what?"

"The School Formal. We can go together. Problem solved. How about it?" Cam grinned at her.

"You're asking me to the dance?" Alice said.

"Well, yeah, I suppose so," Cam said.

Alice looked at him, her face utterly impassive and unreadable. Then she slowly, deliberately, picked up her pasta bowl and, without saying a word, stood up and emptied the contents of the bowl on to his head, before storming out of the dining room.

"I'll take that as a 'no' then, shall I?" Cameron called after her as he picked the pasta spirals out of his hair.

He turned back to Emily and Georgie. "What did I say?"

Georgie shook her head and handed him a napkin. "Here," she said, "you've got tomato sauce on your forehead."

"I don't understand," Georgie said as they walked the horses out to the arena for Tara Kelly's cross-country lesson that afternoon. "You want to go with Cam, don't you?"

"Of course I do!" Alice said, "but I'm not going to be his date just because Kennedy Kirkwood turned him down. You know, Georgie, I've got my pride too. I'm not going to be his fall-back option."

"So do you think Kennedy was making it up?" Georgie asked. "You know, that stuff about already having a date?"

"Kennedy may cheat, but she doesn't lie," Alice said. "She's probably hooked some poor polo boy into taking her."

Kennedy was obviously making plans for the formal; she and Arden were loudly discussing prom dresses as the eventing class lined up for their gear inspection.

"I can't decide between the Victoria Beckham dress or the Marchesa," Arden was complaining.

"You're going off the peg?" Kennedy wrinkled up her nose. "Patricia is getting Fabien to design something especially for me, with lots of Swarovski crystals all over the bodice and—"

"Miss Kirkwood? Miss Mortimer?" Tara Kelly interrupted. "If you girls want to waste valuable time talking about something as unimportant as the School Formal, then you can do it elsewhere – not in my class!"

"Sad old spinster," Arden muttered under her breath as their instructor walked away. "Just because Hans dumped you before the Formal a million years ago, doesn't mean the rest of us are losers too!"

"You're such a numnah, Arden!" Georgie hissed.

Arden's smirk disappeared. "Gee, Georgie," she said sarcastically, "I suppose someone needs to stand up for the lame and the dateless amongst us. And who better to do it than you?"

"That is a joke coming from you, Arden!" Alice said, leaping to Georgie's defence. "Georgie would still have a date if you hadn't stolen her boyfriend."

"I didn't *steal* James!" Arden pouted and glared at Georgie. "You just can't handle the fact that he likes me and not you."

"And you don't think it's a bit weird?" Georgie shot back, "that one minute he's kissing me and the next you're going out with him and he won't even talk to me?"

"That's not how it happened…" Arden began, but she was interrupted by Kennedy.

"Georgie, Georgie, Georgie…" Kennedy shook her head, "you just don't get it, do you? My brother is a Kirkwood – which makes him a Thoroughbred. And Thoroughbreds do not go out with little cart ponies like you. James came to his senses. Get over it and stop drooling over him in the dining hall."

As the riders made their way down to the steeplechase course, the showjumperettes were laughing and giggling and Georgie felt herself shaking with suppressed fury.

"The course is far more slippery than it was last time," Tara told them. "So please, take it easy out there and give each other some space, OK?"

As Georgie drew up to the start line, she tried to regain

her composure. Beneath her, Belle was skipping and dancing with excitement and Georgie turned the mare around to keep her moving until Tara gave the words. "Ready, set, go!"

Belle broke fast, her hind legs propelling her like a racehorse from the start gates, mud flying up from beneath her hooves as she began to gallop.

Georgie stayed with the mare, trying not to fight or hold her back. They were in the middle of the field, and Belle was settling nicely into her rhythm when it began.

Kennedy Kirkwood appeared at Georgie's side. She must have ridden hard to reach Georgie because at the start line she'd been almost on the other side of the group. Now she was right up against Georgie, her chestnut gelding so close to Belle that the two horses only had a narrow space between them. Kennedy rode shoulder to shoulder with Georgie and then, in one insane manoeuvre, she kicked on and yanked her right rein hard, edging out in front and pulling her horse over so that they were barrelling into Georgie's path, cutting her off!

Belle gave a panicked squeal and skidded to the side and Georgie braced herself to keep from flying out of the saddle as she was flung sideways.

"What do you think you're doing?" she screamed, but Kennedy ignored her. Georgie straightened Belle back up again and pushed the mare on. They were just a few strides out from the first jump when once again she was side by side with Kennedy.

It was like a game of chicken. Neither girl would pull off target and admit defeat. They were just two strides out from the fence when Georgie came to her senses. This was madness! It wasn't safe to take the jump with Kennedy alongside her. And it wasn't worth getting herself or her horse injured. She was about to pull Belle back and let Kennedy go in front when a heavy blow struck the mare hard on her shoulder. Kennedy had just ridden right into Belle on purpose!

The sudden impact made Belladonna slip and the wet ground had no purchase – the mare went into a skid. As Georgie felt Belle go over, she did the only thing she could do and flung herself clear of the saddle, trying to get out of Belle's way so she wouldn't be crushed beneath her.

The mud rushed up and Georgie went down hard, face-first. Belle had fallen right beside her and was over on her side, legs flailing as she tried to stand up.

"Easy, girl," Georgie got quickly to her feet and grabbed the reins, trying to stay clear of Belle's hooves as the mare thrashed about. After Belle stumbled to her feet, Georgie led the mare forward, looking for signs of lameness. Belle seemed to be OK and so she began to lead the mare back across the field towards the stables. There was no point in mounting up again – the other riders were long gone and Georgie and Belle's confidence were shattered by the fall.

She could see Tara Kelly walking towards her with a grim expression on her face.

"Is she all right?" Tara asked.

Georgie nodded. "Put her away and then meet me in the tack room," Tara said stiffly, without looking Georgie in the eye.

Georgie sat down at the table in the tack room and waited. Tara had looked so furious out there on the field. But surely she'd seen the way Kennedy cut her off at the start of the race? She must know it wasn't Georgie's fault.

The tack room door flew open and Tara entered. Kennedy Kirkwood was with her.

"Sit down next to Georgie, please, Kennedy," Tara said. She walked around and stood on the other side of the table, facing the two girls, her arms crossed at her chest. "The display I have just witnessed out there has no place on the cross-country course. I don't know what you two were thinking, barging into each other like that and frankly I don't want to hear it. That sort of behaviour is inexcusable. This is cross-country – not dodgems!"

"Kennedy cut me off!" Georgie began to protest.

"No, I didn't!" Kennedy shot back. "She started it!"

Tara held up a hand. "And I'm going to finish it." She looked at the two girls. "You are both on fatigues – I want you mucking out the stables for a week."

"But Miss Kelly!" Kennedy began. But Tara silenced her.

"You should consider yourself lucky that is your only punishment, Miss Kirkwood."

The girls both stood up to go, but Tara wasn't finished. "Georgie, wait."

Georgie turned around as Kennedy walked out and suddenly she knew what was coming.

"I'm sorry, but today was the last assessment class of the term. Georgie, I hate to say this, but I'm afraid your performance has left me no choice."

"But it wasn't my fault," Georgie said as tears started to pour down her cheeks. "I didn't get a chance to ride properly..."

Tara swallowed loudly then broke the news. "Today was your last cross-country class, Georgina. I'm sorry, but you've been eliminated. You're out."

Chapter Fourteen

Georgie knew that there must be worse things in the world than being kicked out of cross-country class. But right now she couldn't think of one. She was devastated. She had come to Blainford with just one goal – to become a professional eventing rider, just like her mum. And now, thanks to Kennedy Kirkwood, that dream was over.

"You have to do something!" Alice was horrified when Georgie finally told her what had happened. "This is so unfair! It wasn't your fault you fell off – Kennedy did it on purpose. You have to tell Tara she's wrong!"

Georgie took a deep breath. "I tried, Alice, but Tara didn't want to know. And I can't prove it was Kennedy's fault. Tara didn't see her push me."

"So," Alice said, "what are you going to do?"

Georgie knew what Alice was driving at. When Georgie's position in the eventing class had been in jeopardy before the mid-term break, she had been on the verge of quitting and leaving Blainford for good.

Now she'd actually been kicked out of Tara's class: the one subject that really mattered to her. She thought of her dad and her best friend Lily and Lucinda and the Little Brampton Stables. If she left Blainford she would be going home, back to her old life and her old school.

"So are you going to… are you gonna go?" Alice asked.

"I thought about it," Georgie admitted, "but it's sort of crazy to throw it all away, isn't it? Besides, we've got the House Showjumping coming up, and I couldn't just leave Belle behind. I lost my horse when I gave up Tyro to come here. I don't think I could stand to say goodbye to Belle too."

Alice let out a sigh of relief. "Oh, good! I mean, I don't think I could cope with having to break in a new room mate. I've kind of got used to you. You're like one of my sisters, only less annoying, you know?"

"Yeah," Georgie smiled. "I know. I feel that way too."

Alice decided that a shopping trip to buy their Formal dresses would help cheer Georgie up. So on Tuesday straight after she had finished her fatigues duty, Alice, Georgie, Emily and Daisy caught the bus from Blainford to downtown Lexington. The journey took them all the way to the centre of town, and from there Alice led the way along Main Street until they reached a side alley signposted Pompadour Lane. There they found Selma's tiny little shop crammed in between a café and a second-hand bookstore.

Inside, there was so much clothing, there was hardly room to move. The racks were jammed full and the air had a musty smell to it. The girl behind the counter gazed up from her book and muttered, "Let me know if you need help," then went back to her novel again.

Alice headed straight for the rails and began to hunt vigorously through the dresses while Georgie milled about without much genuine conviction. She wasn't even sure why she was here. She still didn't even have a date for the Formal so why did she need a dress?

"I bet Damien wants to ask you," Emily insisted, "except he'd get it in the neck from Conrad, wouldn't he? Those polo boys totally hate us more than ever since we beat them in the House Showjumping."

Georgie knew Damien didn't really fancy her. He was only being friendly. But at least he smiled at Georgie and said hello, which was more than any of the other Burghley boys would do.

Conrad's dislike of Georgie had now reached epic proportions. On the way back from dinner she would hear him trailing along behind her on the driveway with the other boys from Burghley House, making childish seagull squawks. Damien was the only one brave enough to ignore Conrad's bullying. As for James, Georgie didn't know what to think. She had caught him staring at her in the dining room the other day. But he was still dating Arden, wasn't he?

"Hey, Georgie!" Alice held out a midnight-blue dress

covered in delicate silver crystal starbursts. "This looks about your size. Try it on!"

The dress had a tight-fitting bodice, tiny shoestring straps and a twisted puffball skirt, and turned out to be a perfect fit. "Wow!" Emily said as Georgie walked out of the tiny fitting room. "You've got to buy it!"

"I don't know…" Georgie looked at herself in the mirror.

"It's brilliant on you," Alice agreed.

Georgie wasn't sure. Maybe her friends were just trying to cheer her up by telling her she looked nice, when really she didn't.

"Daisy?" Georgie turned to the one member of their group who always spoke with brutal bluntness. "What do you think?"

Daisy looked the dress up and down. "It makes you look like you've got boobs and the colour matches your eyes," she said. "You should buy it."

The girl behind the counter informed Georgie that it was an original Betsey Johnson from 1984 and the price was twelve dollars. Georgie still had enough change left over to buy a pair of black ballerina flats and grab a burger before they caught the bus home again.

On the bus, the girls compared purchases. Alice had ferreted out a very pretty violet-coloured prom dress with a full fifties skirt with stiff tulle underneath. Emily, after much umming and ahhing, had settled on a chic one-shouldered black dress and Daisy had stunned everyone by appearing from the changing rooms looking like a supermodel in a vintage Donna Karan gold silk maxi dress.

"I still can't believe we're dateless," Alice sighed as the bus rumbled back towards Blainford. "It's like, incredible to me!"

"Ummm, Alice?" Emily looked nervous. "I hate to tell you, but…" She bit her lip. "I'm not dateless."

"You? Who? When?" Alice was totally stunned.

Emily flushed pink. "Alex Chang finally asked me. He came around to the boarding house while you guys were at showjumping training. He even bought me flowers!"

"Right," Alice said. "OK, well, good for you, Emily. That's great."

She turned to Georgie. "This changes nothing. There's still two of us. We can go together!"

Georgie decided that Alice was right. OK, so Riley had turned her down and didn't want to come to the dance. Big deal! She and Alice would go together. They'd have a brilliant time. "Girl Power!" Georgie giggled.

"Girl Power," Alice agreed.

Their newfound solidarity against the boys of the world lasted exactly ten minutes. That was how long it took them to arrive back at school where Matt Garrett bowled up to Alice on the driveway and asked if she would go to the dance with him.

"I said yes," Alice reported with a beaming grin.

"What?" Georgie sputtered. "What happened to Girl Power?"

"Oh, yeah," Alice looked sheepish. "Sorry about that, Georgie."

"And what about Cam?" asked Georgie.

"Maybe if I go with Matt it will teach him not to take me for granted," Alice said.

"So you're using Matt as a pawn in your game?" Georgie said. "That's not very nice, Alice."

"Oh, come on!" Alice looked at her in disbelief. "Have you met Matt Garrett? He's the most arrogant guy in the whole school. He's so thick-skinned he won't care why I'm going to the Formal with him – he just wants a date."

"It's official then," Georgie groaned. "I am the only loser in the whole school."

On Wednesday, Tara Kelly's showjumpers arrived at the indoor arena for their final training session before the big event. The showjumping finals were to be a three-way competition between Luhmuhlen, Badminton and Adelaide.

"This time there's no safety net," Tara told them. "There are no discard scores. All six riders will be counted in the final tally, so we cannot afford a single mistake from any of you." Tara looked at her clipboard. "I'm going with the same running order as last time. The competition gets underway at eleven thirty and I want you all tacked up and at the arena by eleven to give us enough time to warm up."

As the riders headed into the arena to begin training, Tara took Georgie aside.

"Can we have a quick word, Georgie?" she asked.

Georgie followed her over to the side of the arena.

"I just wanted to tell you how very sorry I am about what happened in cross-country class," Tara began. Georgie nodded. She knew what Tara was saying was true.

"Georgie," Tara continued, "I want you to know that I still think you are one of the brightest talents to emerge amongst the students here at Blainford. And I don't want you to give up, OK? See this as a challenge – not the end of your eventing career. I know that sounds odd, after what has happened, but sometimes these setbacks can be a blessing in disguise. You understand?"

"I... I think so," Georgie said.

Tara smiled. "So are you and I OK? You're still happy to be part of my showjumping team?"

Georgie nodded again. "We're good."

"Excellent," Tara said. "You're my anchor, Georgie. I'm

relying on you to come in at the very end and bring home a clear round. The team needs you."

"You can count on me, Tara," Georgie replied.

As Tara and Georgie entered the showjumping arena, Kendal was warming up around the showjumps.

"OK, Kendal," Tara said. "Off you go, let's see how Shalimar handles the treble."

Kendal was halfway around the course and coming in towards the treble, when Georgie noticed Hans Schockelmann striding across the arena towards Tara.

"Tara, darling!" Hans waved at her. Tara stiffened at the sight of him.

"Hans, I'm going to have to ask you to leave," she said. "We're in the middle of team training."

"Really?" Hans said. "Do you mind if I watch?"

"Yes, I do!" Tara looked at him with an incredulous expression on her face. "You're the opposition!"

"Tara," Hans shook his head, "I don't think of you as competition."

He smiled at her. "There's no way you're going to beat

my Adelaide girls – so why don't you at least take advantage of my help while I'm here? I am the world's number one ranked showjumper after all. It's not every day that Hans Schockelmann turns up and offers to give a free lesson to a group of Blainford pupils."

Tara looked at him in disbelief. "You always were a patronising egomaniac, Hans," she said. "Even when we were at school together."

Hans gave Tara a dark smile, clearly pleased that he had managed to ruffle her demeanour. "As I recall, Tara, you rather liked my egotism then."

"Well, I'm over it now!" Tara snarled. She looked him dead in the eye. "If you're so confident about winning the House Showjumping, how about a little wager then?"

Hans frowned. "Tara, I have no problem taking you up on your little bet, but I am certain it would be against Blainford rules for teachers to put money on their students."

"Who said anything about money?" Tara replied. "I can think of a far more fitting bet between us."

"Name it," Hans said.

"The School Formal is two weeks from now on Saturday

night," Tara said. "The loser has to perform a break-dance in front of the whole school."

Hans' smirk disappeared. "You're kidding."

"Do I look like I'm joking?" Tara said.

Hans nodded. "OK," he said, "you've made your point – you're still bitter about the Formal, I get that."

"I'm not bitter," Tara said, "I'd just like to see you break-dance – that's all."

Hans glared at her. "OK, we will have your little bet. I hope you are ready to lose."

"Oh, I'm not losing," Tara said. "And if I were you, Hans, I'd leave this arena right now and go home and start throwing shapes."

Tara had a confident smile on her face as she watched Hans walk off across the arena. But when she turned back to her team she wasn't smiling.

"Right!" their trainer said. "This is our last training session so let's not waste any more time."

She fixed a steely gaze on the girls. "In case I haven't already made myself clear, I intend to go out there and take it to Adelaide and Luhmuhlen this weekend… This is the House Showjumping finals – and we're riding to win."

Chapter Fifteen

The scarlet shirts of Badminton House marked Georgie, Alice and Daisy out from the rest of the first years as they walked up the driveway on Saturday morning.

"I don't know why we even came," Alice complained as she sat staring at the bacon and eggs that were congealing on her plate. "I'm way too nervous to eat."

"Do you mind if we join you?" The girls looked up to see Cameron and Alex standing there holding their breakfast trays.

"Sure," Alice said, "as long as you tell us your team's secret tactics for the finals."

"Ahhh," Cameron said. "Can't do that, I'm afraid. In fact our captain sent us over here to get your tactics."

"You're kidding!"

"Not really," Alex smiled. "The team wanted us to come over and talk to you, and Cameron agreed because he thought it would give him a chance to apologise to Alice for being such a numnah about the dance."

Cameron glared at Alex. "That was a private plan! You're not supposed to tell the girls the plan!"

"Oh," Alex shrugged. "Sorry."

"Well, at least you're all riding," Emily said. "I'll be on the sidelines not knowing who to cheer for – Badminton or Luhmuhlen."

"What?" Alex looked upset. "You're cheering for me, of course. I'm your boyfriend!"

The others looked at him in astonishment. They knew Alex was taking Emily to the ball, but not that things had progressed to boyfriend/girlfriend status.

"Alex," Cameron shook his head in amazement. "You're just full of information this morning. Maybe we'd better go back to our team table before you give away all our secrets."

"No," Alice smiled at Cam. "Stay."

"You're not going to throw food on my head again, are you?" Cam asked.

"Nah," Alice said. "I'm not wasting a good breakfast."

"Yeah," Georgie agreed. "You need to keep your strength up so we can beat these boys in the showjumping ring."

Emily frowned. "I hope this showjumping competition isn't going to come between us. We're still in eventing class together, remember?"

"Not all of us," Alex said, nodding at Georgie as he munched on a piece of wholemeal toast. "And another one of us will probably get the chop next term."

The others stared at him in disbelief and Cam reached over and picked up Alex's glass of orange juice and gave it a suspicious sniff. "Man, what have they put in this? Truth serum or something?"

"Well," Alex shrugged. "I'm right, aren't I? I mean, if she got rid of Georgie, then no one is safe."

"It's only an eventing class," Alice said. "Not life or death."

"OK," Daisy said to her. "You quit then."

Alice went quiet. "Exactly," Daisy said. "It might not be life and death. But it's what we're all here for."

She looked at Georgie. "I'm sorry, but it's true, isn't it?"

Georgie looked down at her breakfast. She used to think Tara's class was the only thing that mattered, that it was her whole reason for being at Blainford, but now… now she wasn't so sure. But whatever her future held, right now Georgie was part of the Badminton House showjumping team and she was determined to get out there today and win.

The girls had two hours to groom and plait up before they were due to meet the rest of the team. Georgie was relieved when she brought Belle in from the paddocks and the mare wasn't caked in mud for once. As she pulled off her rugs she could see that the clip she had given Belle was already growing back again and her shorn belly had a fuzzy feeling to it.

Georgie worked briskly, beginning with Belle's body and then moving on to do her plaits. When she was done with the mane she wound white tape around the plaits again, but on Belle's legs she swapped to red tape on the gamgee bandages to match Badminton's house colours. The mare looked amazingly glossy and shiny considering it was her winter coat. Georgie had even put quarter-markings on her rump – a diamond pattern that had been brushed into her coat and then hairsprayed to keep it in place.

"Are you ready?" Alice led Will out of his loose box and tied him up alongside Belle.

"Yep," Georgie said, painting the last bit of hoof oil on to Belle's near hind. "I just need to tack up."

The two girls walked together to the tack room. Their gear was stored on saddle racks at the side of the room, and as soon as Georgie caught sight of her saddle she could see something was attached to it. A white envelope had been sellotaped on to the stirrup leather. Georgie ripped it off. Her name was written on it in green pen.

"What's that?" Alice asked.

"I don't know," Georgie said as she opened the envelope. Inside there was a letter, handwritten in the same green pen:

Georgie,
I know things have been weird between us since the

holidays, but I want you to know that I still really care about you. It's over with me and Arden – that was a big, fat mistake. I want you back, Georgie. Please, I need to talk to you. Come and meet me before the showjumping, down at Drover's Dell. If you don't come then I'll know it's really over – James.

Georgie was incapable of speaking. She handed the letter to Alice, whose eyes widened as she read it.

"Ohmygod, Georgie," she said. "Do you want to get back with him too?"

"I don't know," Georgie answered. "Yes, no... kind of..."

"He says he wants you to meet him at Drover's Dell before the showjumping," Alice pointed out. "It's already nearly eleven now!"

Georgie lifted up her saddle, grabbed the bridle off the rack and headed for the door.

"Georgie," Alice said nervously. "Where are you going?"

"Where do you think?" Georgie said. "I'm going to meet James."

"But Georgie!" Alice's voice was filled with panic. "We're due at the arena."

"You go," Georgie insisted as she flung the saddle on to Belle's back. "Tell Tara I'm going to be a little late, but I'll be there for my round."

"You're kidding! Tara will kill you when she finds out!"

"Then she'd better not find out," Georgie said. She cinched up the girth and slipped the bridle over Belle's head. "Listen," she told Alice. "I'm the last one to go in the team, right? That means there'll be all of you guys and the Luhmuhlen and Adelaide riders before me – I won't be due to ride for ages. It takes no time at all to get to Drover's Dell from here. I can talk to James and come back again before the competition has even got going."

"Yeah, but what if he convinces you not to come back?"

"Alice," Georgie said firmly. "I'm coming back. I'll be at the arena in time to ride. You just have to cover for me for a little while, OK?"

The grass verge that ran alongside the oak trees on the driveway from the school to the front entrance gates was wide enough to trot a horse. Georgie had to keep ducking underneath the lower branches from time to time, but even so she didn't lose stride, keeping Belle to a steady rhythm. She knew she shouldn't be doing this. It was irresponsible charging off at the last minute just before the competition was about to get underway, but she knew she could make it. Besides, the trot would loosen Belle up. The mare would be warmed up and ready to compete by the time they arrived back at the showjumping arena. Georgie would just have to pop her over a practice jump or two and they'd be fine.

Georgie looked at her watch. It was eleven-fifteen. She could see the gates up ahead and not far beyond was the grove of trees, Drover's Dell. She just hoped that James was still there, that he hadn't given up on waiting and left already.

"James?" she called out. There was no answer as she headed into the trees, down one of the narrow winding paths. Several of these paths wound their way through the woods, intertwining back and forth across each other before they all came out again on the other side of the copse. It was possible that James was on a different path from her, but the woods were only tiny. He should be able to hear her no matter where he was.

"James!" she yelled out again. "I'm here. Where are you?"

She was almost in the centre of the woods when she saw something moving, just a flash of a horse-shape in the shadows, to her right, out of the corner of her eye.

"James!" she called out again, "I'm over here!" She was certain now that the shape had been a horse – she could hear hoofbeats and the sound of a rider, pushing back branches to fight his way through the trees.

And then she realised something strange. The rider and the horse had been moving through the trees – *but not towards her*. They'd been going around, circling her. And now they'd gone back out of the woods and were heading towards the school gates. Georgie heard horse shoes chiming on metal and then, the sound of the heavy wrought-iron gates, creaking and moaning as they swung shut!

"Hey!" Georgie called out, "don't close those gates! I'm

still out here!" She turned Belle around and trotted the mare as fast as she dared, back along the narrow path between the trees, the way she had come. As she emerged into the sunlight, she blinked and adjusted to the brightness. Ahead of her she could see that the gates had been drawn shut. But the rider on the other side wasn't who she'd been expecting at all.

"Hello, sweetheart," Conrad Miller said as he turned the key in the lock. "Thanks for coming."

Back at the showjumping arena, Tara Kelly was less than impressed to hear that a member of her team wasn't turning up on time.

"What's she doing that's more important than this?" Tara snapped at Alice.

"She... ummm... she had an appointment she couldn't cancel. But she's not far away. She'll be here by eleven thirty," Alice said.

"She better be," Tara said. "Or I'll have her guts for garters!"

As Tara stalked off to go and talk to the rest of the

team, Alice noticed Kennedy Kirkwood smirking at her.

"What is it, Kirkwood?"

"Why didn't you just tell her the truth?" Kennedy said. "Why didn't you tell Tara that Georgie had gone off to meet her so-called boyfriend?"

Alice froze. "How do you know where she's gone?"

"Oops," Kennedy gasped in mock concern. "I shouldn't have said that, should I?"

"What do you know about this, Kennedy?" Alice was furious.

"I know where she's gone because I'm the one who wrote her the note."

"That is so lame," Alice said. "Georgie will just turn around again when there's no one there to meet her."

"Who said," Kennedy purred, "that there's no one to meet her?"

"Please, Conrad!" Georgie was begging now. "You've got to let me back in!"

"Sorry, Parker," Conrad said. "No can do. You'll have to wait out there until the competition is over."

He stood on the other side of the gates, the gate keys dangling from the loop in his hand, just temptingly out of reach.

"Conrad," Georgie tried to reason with him. "You're not even in the competition any more."

Conrad stepped up to the bars. "We should be!" He glared at Georgie. "Burghley House has been in every House Showjumping final for the past twenty-three years. You ruined our record."

"It's a bit late for that now!" Georgie pointed out. "Keeping me from the finals won't win you back the trophy!"

"No," Conrad agreed, "but this way at least Kennedy will win it for Adelaide. Which is better than you losers in Badminton House getting your hands on it."

Of course! Georgie realised at last. Now she knew who was taking the red-haired super-witch to the Formal! It was too awful, but it all made sense at last. Kennedy Kirkwood was dating Conrad Miller.

Chapter Sixteen

"Conrad Miller is your boyfriend?" Alice pulled a face. "No wonder you wouldn't tell us who was taking you to the Formal. I'd keep it quiet too if I was going out with a numnah like Conrad!"

Kennedy's smirk disappeared.

"I'm telling Tara what you've done," Alice continued. "You're so in big trouble."

"I'm not the one who's in trouble," Kennedy countered. "Georgie is already on a warning for being out of bounds. Mrs Dubois told her that if she got caught outside again she'd have all her weekend leave suspended."

"Tell Conrad to let her back in then!" Alice demanded.

"Sure," Kennedy said. "I'll do that just as soon as he gets back. Of course, by then it's going to be too late for

Georgie to compete in the showjumping. The finals will be over and you'll have lost..."

"Alice Dupree!" It was Tara Kelly calling her. "Alice!"

Tara had a face like thunder. "You're due in the arena now. What are you doing?"

"I'm... I'm sorry, Tara," Alice said.

"What is wrong with you girls today?" Tara was exasperated. "You should have been warming up instead of talking to Kennedy. And where on earth is Georgie?"

Georgie Parker was precisely where Conrad Miller had left her, on the wrong side of the front gates of Blainford Academy. Despite her pleas and, in the end, her threats, Conrad had left her there. He'd pocketed the keys and ridden back up the driveway towards the school, ignoring her cries. Georgie sat on her horse, trapped on the other side of the wrought-iron gates, feeling like a complete and utter fool. *Why hadn't she realised that Kennedy and Conrad were behind the letter?* She realised now how completely ridiculous and irresponsible it had been to abandon her team and race off to meet James right before the competition. Kennedy and Conrad might have set this up, but it was her stupid fault for falling for it! She had let Tara down and she had let Badminton House down. And now here she was, locked out and helpless with the clock ticking.

The really frustrating thing was that Georgie could actually see the showjumping competition taking place in the distance. If she looked across the post-and-rail fences, grazing paddocks and the outlying cross-country course, she could just make out the arena where the showjumps were set up. Her team mates would be waiting for her to turn up. Only she wasn't going to.

It was unbearable. Sitting there on Belle, forced to watch as their chances slipped away. They must be almost halfway through the competition by now. If only someone would turn up to open the gates. But everyone was already on the sidelines, watching the showjumping. There was no way she was getting back in through those gates now.

And then it came to her. She couldn't get in through the gates, but there was another way.

"Come on, Belle." Georgie turned the mare away and headed back towards Drover's Dell.

She rode Belle into the woods and back down the same narrow path they'd followed earlier, looking for James. They trotted through the trees, Georgie ducking and swerving beneath the branches as she negotiated the narrow track, until they emerged on the other side of the dell.

On the edge of the woods, a wide grass verge ran alongside the road next to the black post-and-rail fence of grounds. Georgie began to circle Belle at a trot. She was figuring out her striding, choosing the perfect spot.

"Get ready, Belle," she told the mare as she urged her into a canter, and stood up in the stirrups in two-point position. "We're going home."

As Georgie circled Belle, she took the mare all the way to the very edge of the grass verge. Belle's hooves struck briefly against the hard tarmac and then Georgie turned the mare as hard as she could so that they were facing straight at the post-and-rail fence.

Clucking the mare on, she rode her head-on at the

fence. There was only room for two very short strides on the grass verge before they reached the fence. Georgie knew she couldn't afford to make a mistake. The rails were a massive metre-sixty high and these school fences were rock solid. They weren't made for jumping – they were made for keeping horses in. There was a moment when Georgie felt fear tying a knot in her belly. But she steeled herself and kicked on. Belle responded to her rider's unswerving determination. The mare never hesitated, taking the post-and-rail fence on a perfect forward stride and landing neatly on the other side before cantering on.

"Good girl!" Georgie gave her a slappy pat as she rocked back up into two-point position again and pushed Belle into a gallop. Their ride for home was still far from over. From here the open grazing pastures were split into two broad fields. There were still more fences to jump as well – and the first of these was coming up fast, another post-and-rail, just like the one before.

As Belle galloped across the pasture, Georgie was aware that the mare's hooves were suctioning deep into the grass. Tara had closed the cross-country course after

Monday's lesson because she was worried about the rain making the ground too soft. There was much more risk of slipping on soggy, wet grass and if Belle lost her footing then she would slide right into the railings. Luckily showjumping studs were already fixed into the mare's shoes, so at least she had some traction.

Georgie realised just how treacherous the ground was as they took the second post-and-rail fence. Belle jumped cleanly enough, but when she landed on boggy mud on the other side she stumbled, tipping her nose almost to the ground. Georgie had kept her seat securely over the fence so was able to sit back and use the reins to pull Belle's head up and stop her from falling any further.

They were galloping once more and Belle was getting strong against the reins. When Georgie tried to steady her back before the next jump the mare fought her, putting her head up and opening her mouth wide, resisting Georgie's hands.

Don't fight her, Georgie told herself. If Belle approached a fence in wet conditions with her nose in the air, it could be lethal. She needed the mare to look ahead at the jump, not struggle against her hands.

Besides, with over a mile to cover to get back to the showjumping arena, she couldn't afford to exhaust the mare by staging an ongoing battle of wills. It was like Riley said – the best way to conserve Belle's energies was to let the mare have her own way and run at her own pace.

So Georgie let the reins slacken off and crouched like a jockey riding trackwork, absorbing Belle's strides and staying with the mare.

As they came up to the next fence, a massive brush that divided the last of the grazing paddocks from the cross-country course, she knew they were going far too fast. Georgie desperately wanted to take a pull on the reins, to slow Belle down. But she resisted the urge. *Let Belle find her own stride*, she thought to herself. *Trust your horse.* They were three strides out from the brush fence when Georgie realised the scale of the jump in front of her. The hedge was utterly massive! It must have been almost a metre-seventy!

If Belle put a foot out of line, suddenly threw in an extra stride, or, worse still, decided to refuse, then there would be no hope for Georgie. She would be thrown headlong at the jump. *Stop thinking the worst,* she told herself. *Look to the next jump and kick on.*

As Georgie approached the brush fence she pushed the fear out of her mind through strength of willpower alone. She gritted her teeth and instead of pulling back in fear she kicked on instead. They flew the hedge in full gallop and as Belle soared through the air, Georgie felt herself becoming a true cross-country rider.

They were out of the grazing paddocks now, but there were still three more fences to clear. A low spar divided one cross-country course from the next, then a stone wall and finally one more post and rail fence before they reached the warm-up arena.

Urging her mare on, Georgie stayed in two-point position and rode both the spar and the wall with as much conviction as the other jumps, not allowing herself to relax and make a mistake now. Just as she had done before, she let Belle gallop freely at her own pace. The mare felt strong, but Georgie noticed a froth of white sweat was building on Belle's neck. She hoped that once they reached the arena the mare wouldn't be too tired to compete. "Come on, Belle," she said, giving her another slappy pat on her wet neck, "Not much further, girl, I'm right here with you."

"Where is she?" Tara Kelly was furious. Badminton House's fifth rider, Karen Lockhart, was about to complete her round in the arena. She would be followed by the last riders from the Luhmuhlen and Adelaide teams, and then, after that, it was Georgie's turn. The only problem was, Georgie still wasn't here.

Alice didn't know what to say. She'd managed to stall and cover for Georgie for as long as she could, but things were getting desperate. Perhaps Alice needed to confess the truth to Tara and tell her where Georgie had gone.

"Daisy!" Tara instructed. "Go back to the stables and see if you can find her! This is crazy! If she doesn't turn up in the next five minutes we're going to have to forfeit the competition…"

"No!" Alice shook her head. "Tara. I know where she is."

"Well?" Tara looked at Alice. "Don't keep us in suspense. Where is Georgie?"

"I'm here!"

Tara Kelly turned around. Galloping towards her, having flown the last post-and-rail fence just as easily as the first, Georgie Parker was back at Blainford.

"What th—" Tara was horrified. "Georgie, what's been going on?"

"Conrad Miller locked me out of the school gates," Georgie panted. "I jumped Belle back in over the fences."

Tara didn't ask for any more information. There was no time. The last of the Luhmuhlen riders had just entered the arena.

"Is Belle sound?" asked Tara.

"She's fine," Georgie said. "She flew the last two fences as if they weren't even there."

"Get down off her," Tara instructed. "Keep her moving and lead her around to cool her down. She needs to get her wind back. There's only one more rider to go and then you're due in the arena."

"So you're going to let me ride?" Georgie asked.

"Georgie, we're currently in the lead by five points,"

Tara said, "and if I don't field a team of six riders, we're eliminated. Of course I'm letting you ride!"

As Georgie led Belle around, Tara gave her directions for the jumps. Georgie hoped that she could remember them – there was no way for her to walk the course this time.

Meanwhile Alice and Daisy were sent off for supplies. They returned with buckets of water and Georgie stripped off the saddle so they could sponge the mare down.

"Alice – make sure you use the sweat scrapers to get the water off," Tara instructed. "Careful, Daisy! Try not to get her leg bandages wet."

The beautiful red and white bandages that Georgie had applied so perfectly were filthy with mud from Belle's wild gallop.

"Never mind how she looks," Tara put a fresh numnah on her and threw the saddle back on. "The main thing is how she feels."

She gave Georgie a leg up. Belle was ready just in time: the last Adelaide rider was about to finish their round.

"You don't need a practice jump," Tara said. "You've already done enough of those to get her here."

She stepped up to Belle and checked the girth again. "Now remember, the corner is tight into the fifth fence, so go wide on the oxer. You only have one fence in hand, so you can only afford to drop one rail."

Both of them knew what a big ask this was. Georgie had just ridden Belle over a mile at a flat gallop, taking massive fences. It was like riding the Grand National and then expecting to take your horse straight into the ring at Olympia and jump a clear round. Did Belle have enough reserves left in her to get around the showjumping course?

"It's up to you, Georgie," Tara said. "Good luck."

As Georgie entered the arena, she caught sight of Kennedy and couldn't help but feel triumphant at the look of surprise on the showjumperette's face. She gave her a nod of acknowledgement as if to say, "That's right – I'm back" and then she rode in to the sound of the cheering from the Badminton House supporters and the ring of the judges' bell.

Georgie looked straight at the first fence and felt the knot in her stomach tighten.

Her nerves tensed as she approached the first jump and she gave in to a moment of panic, holding Belle back. The mare fought against Georgie's hands and stuck her head in the air, mistiming the jump. She leapt from too far out and Georgie heard the loud "ohhhh" from the crowd as Belle knocked the top rail of the first fence with her hind legs.

It had fallen! She'd already got four faults! There were no more chances now. If they were going to win, then from here on in they had to go completely clear.

Georgie tried to block out the pressure and noise of the crowd. *You can do this*, she told herself. *Focus!*

Belle was still remarkably fresh after her wild gallop and it had taken that first fence for her to realise that she was in the showjumping arena. Now, the mare seemed to settle down and listen to Georgie.

Don't use you hands, steady her back with your seat, Georgie thought, remembering Riley's advice. She sat back and looked for the stride into the second jump and this time Belle put in a perfect stride to clear the jump beautifully. The Badminton supporters let out a cheer.

At jumps three and four Georgie was back in control. Belle was alert and listening, popping them neatly. Georgie remembered what Tara had told her just in time as she came to the oxer, swinging wide enough to get in two perfect strides, and taking the fence cleanly. Then they were on and over the next three jumps with no problems.

The very last fence loomed ahead of them. The jump was a big one. But to Georgie, who had just jumped a metre-seventy brush fence, it looked like a piece of cake.

Belle didn't hesitate and arced the jump beautifully. Then Georgie was leaning low over the mare's neck and urging her on, well within the time, to the finish flags ahead. The crowd were on their feet and going berserk as Georgie, exhausted and elated, raised a fist in victory and punched the air. They had four faults and that was good enough for glory. Badminton had won the House Showjumping!

Chapter Seventeen

Georgie adjusted the straps on her midnight-blue dress and stepped back to look at herself in the mirror.

"Do you think I should wear a necklace or something?" She cocked her head to one side as she stared at her reflection.

"Ohhh!" Alice leapt up from her bed. "I know what you can wear with it!"

She ran over to her dressing table and grabbed a red silk sash with gold lettering, and tied it across Georgie's shoulder. "Perfect!"

Georgie giggled, "It's not a beauty pageant!"

"We should all wear them," Alice said. "You know, if Adelaide House had won I bet they'd wear their House Showjumping sashes to the Formal."

Georgie had won a lot of ribbons and rosettes over the years, but she had never been more proud than she was when Mrs Dickins-Thomson tied the red winner's sash around Belle's neck. It was the best fun ever doing the victory lap of the showjumping course, Georgie leading the team as they waved to the crowd.

By now the whole team knew why Georgie had been late. Her heroic dash across country was quickly becoming part of the legend that would go down in Badminton House history.

Once the competition was over, Georgie told Tara Kelly the whole story of what had happened too. Tara had listened, a serious expression on her face, and when Georgie finished she thought for a while before she spoke. "I can take up the matter with Mrs Dickins-Thomson," Tara said, "but I'm afraid it will be very much your word against Conrad Miller's. And since he is a prefect, and you were out of bounds, you might actually end up in trouble yourself."

The unfairness of this, and the fact that Kennedy was

going to get away with sabotaging her once again, infuriated Georgie and the rest of the Badminton House girls. Still, at least Tara Kelly believed her.

"She knows it wasn't your fault," Alice consoled her.

"But it was," Georgie replied. "If I hadn't blown the whole James thing so out of perspective, then I would never have fallen for it. I should have known he'd never write a note like that. I think in my heart I just didn't want to admit that it was fake."

Looking back, Georgie still didn't know what went wrong between her and James. But whatever had happened, it was over and done with now.

Anyway, she didn't regret her wild ride across the Blainford grounds. It was like everything had come together when she was riding Belle that day. She hadn't tried to fight the mare and had just let her run, and something inside Georgie had clicked. She understood Belle now – and knew exactly how to handle the mare on the cross-country course.

Georgie never thought she would be looking forward to the Formal, but tonight she felt she deserved a chance to let her hair down.

But first she had to put her hair up. "Ummphh, hold still!" Alice was struggling with three hairbands and a mouth full of hairpins.

"Oww! You stabbed me!" Georgie winced as Alice shoved a pin in to secure her blonde hair in a cute, messy chignon.

Alice stood back to admire her efforts. "It'll have to do," she said. "We're late."

"Just as well we weren't competing against the clock this time," Daisy groaned as Georgie and Alice finally joined her and Emily at the front door.

Usually the Badminton House girls made the long walk up the school driveway in jodhpurs and riding boots. But tonight there were giggles as they negotiated the road in the moonlight in precariously high heels and sparkling dresses.

They'd arranged to meet the boys under the archway at the front of the quad. Matt, Alex and Nicholas were already there waiting for them, along with Cameron, who was dateless, like Georgie.

"You'll see. Going solo isn't so bad," he told her as they walked towards the hall. "If you play your cards right, I might even save a dance for you."

"Gee, really Cam? Thanks!" Georgie said sarcastically.

The Formal was being held in the Great Hall and the seniors, including Kendal, who was on the social committee, had been in charge of the decorations, which had an autumnal theme. The doorway to the Great Hall was strung with gold and white fairy lights, and inside there were more lights strung over gigantic papier mâché maple trees, their carnelian leaves covered with a faint dusting of sparkling white fake snow.

"I know," Kendal groaned, "it's cheesy, right?"

"No," Georgie said. "No, really, I think it looks beautiful."

They were walking through the trees and Georgie was leading the way to the drinks table when Alice reached out and grabbed her by the arm. "Uh-oh," she said. "Maybe we should get our drinks later?"

Georgie looked up and saw what had made Alice hesitate. Standing in front of the punchbowl was James Kirkwood. He was by himself, holding a drink, and when he saw Georgie he waved at her, beckoning her over.

"Forget about him, Georgie," Alice said. "Why don't we go and dance with Cam and Matt instead?"

"No," Georgie said. "It's OK, Alice. You go dance. I'm going to talk to James."

"Really?" Alice looked worried. "Do you want me to come with you?"

"No," Georgie said. "Thanks, Alice, but I need to do this on my own."

As Georgie walked across the floor to James, she realised it was the first time for ages that they had been face to face like this.

"I heard what happened at the showjumping finals," James said. "You know, about the note and stuff."

Georgie felt herself blushing. Great! So James knew that she'd gone galloping off to meet him when he wasn't there.

"Well, Kennedy can be quite convincing," Georgie stuttered. "The note said you'd split up from Arden and you wanted to see me. I know that sounds stupid but—"

"It doesn't sound stupid," James replied. "I have split up with Arden."

Georgie was shocked. James dug into the pocket of his suit jacket and pulled out a piece of paper. "When I heard about what Kennedy had done, I realised that maybe I'd been wrong about some things too," he said.

He handed the piece of paper to Georgie. "Here. Read it."

It was just like the note Kennedy had written to Georgie, in the same green pen with the exact same handwriting:

James
I am officially breaking up with you. Your kisses are so slobbery I'd rather stick my tongue down the throat of one of your dad's hounds. You think you are a really genius rider, but I'm so much better than you. This has been the worst holiday of my life and I hope that when we get back to Blainford I never have to speak to you again.
Georgie.

As Georgie read on, her eyes widened in horror.

"James!" she said, "I never, I mean, I would never have sent this! It's not mine!"

"Well, yeah, I know that now," James said. "But when I found this letter in my room that night I didn't know what to think. Then Dad asked if I wanted to go to New York with him and..."

"I get it," Georgie said, still examining the letter in stunned disbelief. "I guess I would have gone too."

James sighed. "I should have figured it out. All that stupid stuff about kissing the hounds – only Kennedy would be that childish. But even for my sister this is beyond uncool."

"She got us both," Georgie said softly.

"So," James stuck his hands in his pockets and looked up at her through his blonde fringe. "What now? Are we going to be friends again?"

Georgie looked serious. "I'm going to have to think about it."

James looked dejected as Georgie turned to walk away. She took two steps and then she spun around again with a grin on her face. "OK, I thought about it!" She laughed, "We're friends again!"

Georgie couldn't wait to tell Alice. She found her standing with Cameron by the buffet and enjoyed the looks of astonishment on their faces as she told them all about Kennedy and the forged letters.

"Holy horse rustlers!" Alice almost choked on a miniature savoury tart. "She's even more of a witch than we thought!"

Georgie nodded.

"Oh, man," Alice shook her head in amazement. "That girl has so got it coming!"

"You know what we should do..." Alice began. But before she could outline a plan, a spotlight suddenly illuminated the centre of the dancefloor.

"What's going on?" Alice asked as Tara Kelly came sweeping into the spotlight with a microphone in her hand and an uncharacteristically large grin on her face.

"Good evening, everyone!" she said. "I have a special

treat in store for you. A little bit of entertainment to get the party started! Performing at Blainford Academy tonight, showing off his legendary break-dancing skills as penance for being the *losing* coach, we have a world-famous showjumping superstar – the one... the only... Hans Schockelmann!"

Tara turned around and pointed a finger at the DJ, who started pumping out hip-hop music. There was whooping and hollering from the crowd and then reluctantly, Hans Schockelmann stepped forward from the edge of the dance floor and into the spotlight. The crowd went wild, applauding and cheering as Hans took a bow and then, grudgingly, with a pained expression and absolutely no good humour whatsoever, got down on the floor and did a backspin. Then he staggered to his feet and launched into the robot. By the time he did the moonwalk to finish off his routine, Cam, Alice and Georgie were laughing so hard they were crying.

"Hey, Georgie," Cameron said as they finally calmed down. "Have you noticed that guy over there is kind of staring at you."

"What are you talking about?"

"By the door," Cameron said. "He keeps looking at you. Do you know him or something?"

Georgie looked up and saw him immediately. He wore a sleek navy suit, and his dark hair was combed back, exposing his high cheekbones and those green eyes. Georgie noticed once again the way his slightly crooked nose made him even more handsome than if it were perfect.

"Riley," Georgie breathed. "It's Riley. He came after all!"

"That's Riley?" Alice nearly choked on her drink. "Georgie! You didn't mention he was gorgeous!"

"I thought I did," Georgie said as she began to walk away.

"Trust me!" Alice called after her. "I would have remembered!"

Riley stood watching Georgie as she walked towards him. "Nice dress," he said with a smile.

"Nice suit," she replied. "I didn't think coming to a dance was your type of thing."

"It's not," Riley admitted. "But then I realised that there are some Blainford students I do like."

"Which ones?" Georgie asked.

"The ones that wear pretty blue dresses and talk too much when they should be dancing," Riley said.

And in one deft move, he spun her on to the dance floor.

"I thought you couldn't dance!" Georgie was amazed.

"I said I didn't dance – I never said I couldn't," Riley smiled as they moved in time. "So how are you and Belle doing?"

"Not so good," Georgie said. "We got kicked out of cross-country class." And he saw the way her lips trembled as she said the words.

"Riley, I don't know what I'm going to do." Georgie's eyes filled with tears. "The only reason I'm at Blainford is to become an eventer and if I can't ride cross-country…"

"Well then," Riley said, "I guess you're just gonna have to find a way to get back in that class again."

The way Riley said this, as if it were the easiest thing in the world, made Georgie suddenly realise that this wasn't over. Kennedy might have taken her place from her in Tara's class – but it was up to Georgie to take it back.

"You're right," Georgie said. "And Belle *is* so much better – we both are. You should have seen the way Belle jumped back over the school fence, Riley – she took a metre-sixty as if it wasn't even there."

"That mare of yours is a special horse," Riley said. He paused and then he said, "Hey, did Kenny tell you that Talisman won his race the day after you rode him?"

"Really?" Georgie couldn't believe it.

"Dad and the boys down at Keeneland are calling you the good luck charm," Riley said. "He wants to know if you'll come back and ride track again next weekend."

Georgie stopped dancing. "Is that why you're here? Did your dad send you?"

Georgie wrenched herself free from his arms and stood there on the dance floor, staring at him defiantly.

"Oh, come on, Georgie!" Riley pleaded, "Don't be crazy!"

"I'm not being crazy," she said. "Why are you here, Riley?"

Riley raked a hand through his hair and stared at the

floor. "Don't make me do this, Georgie. I'm no good at this romance stuff…" he mumbled uncomfortably. "This was a mistake, me turning up here like this. I'm sorry, I…"

But he didn't get a chance to finish because Georgie suddenly shocked everyone in the hall, including herself, by planting a kiss on him.

"I'm no good at the romance stuff either," she breathed as she pulled away and stood in front of him once more, her heart racing.

Riley smiled. "Well then," he said, putting his arms around her and drawing her close. "I guess we just need to practise."

STACY GREGG

When Georgie's dreams of becoming a
world-class eventing rider suffer a setback
she must beat her rivals at a whole new game
– polo. The Blainford Academy polo team are
competing for the Bluegrass Cup and Georgie
is pitted against an unexpected foe.
Meanwhile, Riley and James are both fighting
for her attention… Who will she choose?

HarperCollins *Children's Books*